MW01244140

Darkness Polished

The Aevarat Galaxy

D.E. Kilgore

Published by D.E. Kilgore, 2021.

This is a work of fiction. Similarities to real people, places, or events are entirely coincidental.

DARKNESS POLISHED

First edition. March 8, 2021.

Written by D.E. Kilgore.

Some stories demand a couple hundred pages to be properly spun,
...others...
Others only ask for a few lines.

ALPHA

Do you even know who I am?
I am the fucking Alpha, number one queen bitch.
Don't come at me with your petty little girl bullshit.
Because if you do, I don't care if you are one of the best fighters here in
this rag tag group you call the order.
I will rip your god forsaken throat out and laugh as you choke to death
on your own blood.
Fuck your Bullshit,
I am Kali, the destroyer of mother fucking worlds,
the destroyer of preconceived notions.
And I will start with you,
don't ever forget that.

Always Watching

I wonder if they know.
Do they know I love to watch them?
Centuries go by being passed, traded, stolen, and sold.
I watched their rise, and I watched their fall.
Always the same, and yet...
I still cannot help but to watch.
Too bad they will never understand how fleeting their race really is,
and how many times they revolved right back to the beginning.
Always Watching,
The Useless Statue in the Corner

Among Us

They have been living among us since the dawn of time.
We always suspected but we thought they were stuff of legend, horror stories, and imagination.
We lived in a world of supernatural beings and horror stories.
Finally, they couldn't hide themselves among us anymore.
The first to come out were the— how is the best way to describe it?
The non-scary ones.
You know, the unicorns, fairies, elves—the pretty ones.
The ones who don't look like monsters.
Then out came all the others.
The vampires, shapeshifters, witches— the rest trickled out slowly after that.
Most species have outed themselves.
We know more still hide in the shadows, but we are not ready for them.
People rioted and killed in the beginning; by the end, world leaders had to come together issuing military rule around the globe.
Fan groups and radicals line every street corner now.
Years passed by before we moved past the fact our stories became reality and eventually adapted as humans are prone to do.
Laws were put in place.
The ones who look human are treated as such.
They live among us now, in the open.
They are our neighbors, our family, our lovers.
I grew up among them.
They go to our schools and they are our friends.

Until—

Until nothing honestly, did you think this was going to be a tragedy?

So, who am I you ask and why am I telling you all of this?

I am no one of significance.

Just your typical bored teenaged girl waiting for detention to end.

Ancient Memories

Once I dreamed.

I dreamed of a world where silver stars floated aimlessly across a midnight sky.

Emerald green grass swayed to the rhythm of the world, sparkling, and dripping with nightly dew as the wind whispered across my bare skin, its hands ruffling through the loftiest trees my eyes had ever beheld.

And when I came upon an iridescent lake, I stared in wonder at the moon reflecting within its glass exterior.

Reaching out, I hesitated, fingers trembling knowing if I gave in to temptation the illusion would shatter into a million pieces beneath my fingertips.

So instead, I closed my eyes and listened to the earth's heart pounding under my feet, a drumbeat echoing to a song long forgotten.

And when my feet took over, swaying and dancing as I never had before, a wildness grew deep down inside of me in need of release.

And when the she-wolf of the moon danced down to me from on high, I knew then I never wanted to leave.

Falling...

Exhaustion finally creeping in as the midnight sky began to lighten, leaves drifting up to the sky, I cried as the she-wolf sang a song so pure, I knew I was not in a dream but instead a memory of a world lost to time itself.

And when I awoke,

I knew reality would never know how they lost a world so beautifully wild.

Beast

The beast in my head always stirred in the early hours of the day, long before daylight broke. Far earlier then I needed to wake for the day but lately, I had come to enjoy these early morning hours. It was during these times, when everything and everyone were still asleep, the beast and I felt most at peace. Some days, we would just sit on a window ledge and watch the world wake up. Other days, the beast and I would pad lightly down to the galley and watch the cooks prepare for the day. It was only during these morning hours I ever felt comfortable enough to let the beast take control. The early morning freedom and once a month run made it complacent for the most part. I was unsure of how long the peace would last within our mind though. I could feel the storm beginning to build up deep within my mind. Soon the storm would break, and my control would snap.

When that day comes, I will have to fight for my life. I am unsure in which one of us will win when that day finally comes.

In the meantime, though, we still had today. Our senses picked up movement down the hall and our ears perked up at the telltale slide of a book leaving its resting place on a shelf.

Creeping towards the massive door leading to the study room, the beast snorted and an image of a tiny room with a stack of books filtered through my mind.

I let out a rare smile.

The beast only ever communicated with me this way, flashes of images. I had no idea if it could speak words and to be honest with myself, I was too scared to ask.

Wouldn't that mean I was just speaking to a voice within my head which no one else could hear? Last time I checked, speaking to the voices in your head was grounds to lock you away for life or worse, be hunted down by the families.

The beast and I threw open the study doors as one and rolled into the room, trying to startle our sister. It never worked, it was like she had her own sense and always knew our location. She always said it was her '*big sister*' senses.

She glanced at me briefly, one brow arched in her patented "*is that all you got*" look.

The beast snorted in my head and we padded over to the windowsill, next to the chair our sister was lounging in. She turned away, continuing to read the massive tome of a book balanced precariously upon her legs. We sat in silence, my sister, the beast, and I. The beast peaked out of my eyes, taking in my sister as she scratched at a piece of paper with an ink quill. The beast was curious but knew better then to interrupt.

Instead, we turned to watch the sun as it slowly began to peak its way out of the darkness and the beast purred, slowly slipping back into the darkness of my mind until it was only me once more.

Best Time of the Year

L eaning over the bathroom counter, she applied the bright red lipstick sitting on the counter. Fluffing her long dark mahogany hair with her perfectly manicured nails, she headed out into the spacious master bedroom, checking herself out in the full-length mirror. She looked drop dead sexy in her little cheerleading costume. Giggling at her little pun, she did a little twirl, admiring the splattering of blood all over her legs and chest.

It was of course on purpose. She didn't want to clash with her extravagant set up downstairs. She squealed, hopping up and down at the chime of the doorbell.

Her first tricker-treaters had arrived!

She hopes they like her decorations. She has after all been planning this all year long. Each year always got better and better. She even impressed herself most days on her budding imagination.

Blowing a kiss to the dog she left on the second-floor balcony, it whined staring at her through the sliding glass door. It was a nice warm night out, so she had no worry of it being uncomfortable. Plus, she couldn't have the yappy little thing scaring away her tricker- treaters, now could she?

Running down the stairs, she grabbed her bloody pompoms from the kitchen island in passing before hopping over the bleeding woman sprawled out on the floor. Her shoes make bloodied footsteps leading up to the massive wood door. Flinging it wide open, she smiles as the little kids scream *"TRICKER TREAT"*, and the blissful sound resonates through her body.

She loves this time of the year.

"Welcome." She says with a haunted voice, "Welcome to my house of horrors!"

Dramatically, she sweeps her arm out and opens the door even wider so the kiddies could see the entirety of her amazing set up. They *woo and ahh*, just as she expected. She hands them candy and waves goodbye, shutting the door.

The bell again! How popular she is already.

She opens the door and gets her *'woos and ahh's'* but wait— a child squeals in excitement and points to the woman on the ground. She looks and laughs as the woman slowly tries to drag herself to the door, blood spilling from her slackened jaw. She gives the squealing children candy once more and waves goodbye before shutting the door. Frowning, she walks over to the woman. As fun as that was, she can't have people catching on. She slams her heel into the back of the woman's head, once, twice, three times. Finally, the skull cracks and brains deposit onto the linoleum floor. She smiles and leans down adjusting the woman's head.

Perfect.

She turns to the muffled yell from behind. Finally, the man of the house is awake. Striding over to him, she puts a little extra sway into her hips, seductively trailing her hand down his body. His eyes widen in fear and he tries to say something, but everything is muffled behind the tape. She gives him a wicked smile, her fingers trailing down over his thigh, and jerks the imbedded hunting knife out of his leg. She enjoys his muffled screams as blood squirts up onto her chest and stomach. He will bleed out soon; she had made sure to hit an artery.

The doorbell rings once again. More kids, more smiles, and squeals of excitement. Soon the candy runs out and she shuts off the outside lights. She turns to look over her masterpiece with pride one last time. An ache of sadness arches through her body at her next thought.

Her time was now over.

With a sigh, she strips and changes before leaving out the back door. Her red mustang convertible was just down the block and she lets out a *purr* at the sound of the engine revving. She is already thinking of next year and her sadness dissipates for the time being. Speeding out of the suburb, she smiles.

Until next year.

Change

His breath hitched, lungs constricting, trying to breathe through the
ache—the pain.
Running, stumbling through the canyon.
He looks to the bloodied moon high above and cries out in agony.
He was changing and he couldn't stop.
He never could no matter how hard he tried.
Stumbling, he falls to his knees,
disturbing the tranquil stream before him.
He doesn't want to change,
not again.
He doesn't want to give up the life he built.
Giving in would mean losing everything he had, everything he always
wanted to be.
He doesn't want to live on the outskirts of society,
of humanity again.
He doesn't want them to see who he really is.
He screams one last time as the change takes over fully.
And for the last time, he reaches up to the sky, hands turned to claws,
howling to the moon knowing there was no coming back.
Not this time.

Control

I stared at the soft beige ceiling of the boarding room, rain pattering against the balconies glass doors. A small whirl sounded in the room next to mine, the air clicking on. I concentrated on the sounds going on around me, trying to ignore the building pressure in the back of my head.

Rolling over, I buried my face into the musty pillow thinking back to what or really who woke up the monster within. We had a deal only to be broken in dire life altering moments and this was definitely not one of those times. A little click sounded, like someone tapping metal on metal and I counted.

One, two, three—eight.

Click.

I growled and rolled out of bed, quickly putting my hair up into a messy bun and shrugged on my utility pants. I always kept my clothes close by because of times like these, which have been getting more frequent. My control was slipping more and more these days, allowing the monster to emerge unexpectedly. It had taken awhile to learn what the pressure in my head meant but once I figured it out, the monster and I made a deal. Though right now that deal seemed null in void to the monster. I learned the hard way long ago, I had no choice when the clicking started— the monster giving me a warning to what was about to come. Reason number one to why I started sleeping in most of my hunting garb, sometimes fully dressed too when too much time elapsed between episodes, and I grew nervous. Snagging my boots, I reached for my jacket just as the time between clicks reached to one count.

Silence.

Shit.

The last word ran through my mind as I felt my control fall away and the monster rose to take over my mind. I watched from within my own head as the monster now rode my body.

I was no longer in control.

The monster bolted through the now open balcony doors, bare feet silently ghosting across the railing, and landing noiselessly onto muddied ground. My feet never made a sound as we moved from shadow to shadow making our way through the marketplace, past the north end of the city, and into the open expanse of the desert before us. A thought skittered across my brain, something about b*oots, feet, and hot sand*; but the sand was not hot in this moment and the monster pushed the thought away with a growl. The moon was full, its light glittering off now silvered eyes, and the monster let out a laugh before pushing its other half into the darkness of their mind.

The monster was fully in control as it sprinted across the sands following the scent trail of the man from the marketplace.

EXHAUSTION RACKED THE monster's human body and a dull throb had begun, starting at the feet, radiating up. The other one—the human half, scrambled for control as this was the longest I had ever hijacked our mind.

That was fine. For I now knew what I was searching for. I let her grab hold of the body as I slowed down and pushed myself back into the darkness.

An echo of a grin radiated throughout my mind from the monster and I wildly grabbed at the ground as I fell forward, fully in control again. I swear I could hear the soft echo of laughter in my head as I took in my surroundings.

This was not good.

I had had an episode, loss of control in another country, with no backup. This shouldn't have happened. Unless—We had been fine, in synch for the last year with no problems. It had made good on our deal until this— until tonight happened. I shivered and sunk my hands into the sand. Something must have triggered the monster, making it go into overdrive. My senses—No our senses must have picked something up in the market. Something or someone who fell into the realm of our agreement. The pressure built up in my head slowly and I shook it off. It grabbed at me again, not like before but in a different way. I knew what it wanted. It wanted to speak to me, but I was not going down that path again, not after what happened last time. I felt the pressure build up like a tidal wave hitting me hard. I swore I heard the word *'fine'* growled in my mind before blackness overtook me once more and I felt my body start to move on its own accord.

BLINK—SUNLIGHT SLOWLY creeped through the darkness, throwing soft light through the emerging landscape. I could make out nothing but brush here and there, and what I liked to call desert trees, peaking out in the distance. I fought for control only to be pushed back once more.

BLINK—I GRABBED FOR control and it let me take over. Surprised, from my other half giving in without a fight, had me falling hard on my knees. Sweat beaded and pooled down my neck soaking into my top. I blinked and swayed looking up to the sun, heat radiating onto my bare arms.

I was going to get a massive sunburn, I thought, followed by an audible snort; sure, that is the first thing I should be thinking about—Sunburn.

My eye lids grew heavy, and I fell back.

BLINK—A MAN IS STANDING before me, blocking out the sun. I squint, looking up at him, trying to make him less fuzzy. He reaches down and I wait for the monster to react, to take control, but nothing happened. The damn thing left me fully in charge and took all its extra abilities I depended on with it.

Thanks a lot, I think groggily, as the man hefts me up into his arms.

The monster rustles briefly in my mind, not even an iota of care about the stranger who just picked me up. A whisper of calmness races through my body and I take my first deep breath, filling my lungs fully with air. It felt like a century had passed since I was last able to do that. The man hugs me closer against his body and whispers as I fall back into darkness.

The Cursed Blades

Steal flashed and thunder crashed, the ground shaking under the town.
People ran, screaming, as our steel, wet from the rain rang loud.
Trapped souls rose like smoke from our blades.
This was never a fight between the wielders,
the poor flesh charmed into picking us up.
No, this fight has always been between the blades.
Centuries passing.
Reason lost to time itself.

Death

Do you think they would celebrate life more freely and
without a doubt if they knew what came after?
If they knew every single one of them was correct
and incorrect at the same time?
What then if they knew?
What would they do?
What would you do?
Do you think you would change your ways?
Or would you scoff in disbelief and continue living without change?
Forever Unwanted,
Death

Desert Warriors

T he desert surrounding us was not always such.

Once long ago, all was freshwater: rolling rivers, endless lakes, and underground caverns filled with the purest water within all the Realms. We lived and thrived in small bands throughout our realm and as with all species, we evolved. Most know of our distant cousins the Ocean Sirens.

Lesser known were the Swamp Sirens. They are all but extinct now, at least within this Realm.

And we were once called River Sirens, though we thrived in any freshwater. It is said the Water Goddess herself was so entranced by the first river siren, she touched us with her magic giving us extra abilities. Although all Sirens exhibited longevity and quick healing, along with our fabled voices entrancing all those around us, the River Sirens in particular, were blessed with the ability to survive outside of the water.

In our early years, we tended to stay near the rivers and other bodies of water, interacting only with others of our kind. Yet when a lone human or other creature crossed our path, we would extend kindness. We were never warriors.

Yet as times changed, humans changed.

Blessed with human likeness outside of water, the beauty of our women and strength of our men became coveted. It was then, we learned the goddess had blessed us once more. We could see the desires of the humans and this would eventually lead to our downfall. We saw what the humans wanted, would take from us and we pulled away. We thought if we hid ourselves away, the humans in turn would forget our coveted ability.

Yet times changed once more, environments altered and slowly, the waters became less and less. We found ourselves needing to interact once again with the humans. Clans separated looking for a new place to call home and it was then, the Dragon Wars began.

We had to choose, to stand against or with the humans. The choice was not as clear as one would think. We tried to negotiate with the dragons who seemingly showed up out of nowhere. Soon, we learned that just like in all species, there are the good and there are the bad. In this instance, the bad outweighed the good and we sided with the humans.

We lost many in the war.

Elders and children, casualties of a war we never wanted to be involved in died, and in turn, certain abilities died with them. When the wars ended, we lost all those who could teach us the ways to harness our voices like our brethren before us and we lost our biggest defense against the humans. We thought them friends—allies after our help with the wars, but instead the humans used us, trapping us into servitude when they learned our only defense against them was lost. Those of us who managed to escape were few and far between. Due to this, our clan found ourselves running back to the only home we ever knew.

We wandered the desert searching for a new home when we stumbled across the Oasis. Other clans—nomads like us, took us in and taught us the ways of the desert. They also taught us a valuable lesson. They taught us how to protect ourselves, to become warriors, and so, the *Ashcrest Family* became the first Siren Clan to become champions of our people. When the humans came for us again, we drove them away and in turn gained fear and respect.

After the destruction of the Dragon Wars concluded, we heard of the families who came out victorious. We decided to stay hidden, to move within the backdrop of society because we learned a few valuable lessons about the humans.

The most dangerous being— resiliency.

We stayed away, hidden until eventually the humans expanded and built permanent settlements. Soon, an unwritten bargain was struck between the small desert settlements and our clan. We protected them, the desert and they left us to be, never to mention our clan to the families.

Overtime the settlement became a city, no longer needing our protection and we became a whisper of a story, a tale told around the campfire. Given time even the city's oldest generation, with family lines stretching back to the wars themselves, thought we all but died out.

Only a few know the truth, how we became protectors of the desert itself and how we still live on the outskirts of the city—waiting for time to show us our future once more.

Diplomacy Fail

"I think it's time we got started then. Would you like a cup of tea?" I shook my head no.

The woman, clearly in charge of the small encampment shrugged and looked to the man at her side, who was still glaring at me. "My brother here found you in the desert a mile away from our camp. Shoeless—no supplies. Just sitting there, looking up to the sky just after dawn. You are a long way from the city, do you care to enlighten us as to why?"

I plastered a smile on my face remembering what my grandfather always said.

Diplomacy is key until you know their angle, play nice; even more so when you are alone without backup in unknown territory.

"Your questions are quite reasonable. As you probably already ascertained, I am just a lone visitor to the city and honestly, I'm not familiar with this region. A series of, now that I think of it, laughable incidents took me out of the city. One thing eventually led to another," I nodded to the man, "and I am incredibly grateful for you finding me. I can be such a ditz sometimes."

The man sighed and crossed his arms. "Has that line ever worked?"

I locked eyes with him once more as the woman beside him sighed. "Helios, really?"

My smiled dropped. "Okay then, Helios is it?"

The man shrugged and I continued. "Truth time. How about this: wrong place wrong time, got a little turned around. I'm just looking to get back to the city. Which is exactly how much I plan on divulging about how and where you found me. Though if you must know, I did not come here or to the city for you or your own."

The woman cocked her eyebrow. "Well, this got off to an awkward start. Perhaps we should try again."

She strode forward, eyes seeming to change from dark brown to emerald green. I blinked and they were back to their normal dark brown once more. A shiver ran its way down my spine as the woman crouched down in front of me. "Hunter, why did you come here? And before you think to lie, I know all about you, your family, and your abilities."

This time it was my eyes which changed, honeyed brown to molten gold. I let the monster within surface with a growl. "Is that so?"

My ears picked up the sound of a sword unsheathing.

That was funny.

My eyes flickered across the features of the woman in front of me, before I leaned to the side taking in Helios, sword in hand. "That's a pretty piece of equipment you have."

If I didn't know any better, I would swear a blush tinted Helios's face at my remark. The woman in front of me cleared her throat, bringing my attention back to her. Before she could say anything more, I leaned backwards and sprung up, joints liquid as I vaulted over the chair backwards. As far as plans went, mine was to dive through the opening of the tent behind me and make my way back to the city so I could report back to the family the beings I tracked down. The thing was—I held up my hands as Helios rushed in, blade to my throat. These beings were much faster than I had anticipated. The monster within chuckled and I let it take over a little more. I wasn't about to let it fully take control. I didn't want a slaughter—at least not yet. Helios's blade was steady at my throat and my monster was impressed. As was I. Not many could face me down with the monster inside this close to the surface.

Maybe—no, he wouldn't have the stones to do it. Energy crackled across my skin and I could feel my canines begin to lengthen. I let the monster speak, my voice changing, lower, more honeyed in tone. "Interesting."

Helios's jaw ticked and I felt the blade bite into my neck slightly. I stretched my head back exposing more of my neck, throwing my hands out to my side. The silence was suffocating as I submitted myself to defeat. Seconds ticked by and a bead of sweat caressed the side of my face before landing on the blade. Slowly, ever so slowly, Helios's arm began to lower.

I was correct, he didn't have the stones.

My closed hand struck out, fist connecting to the soft flesh of his throat. His reaction was a hairs breath too slow as I bent backwards, blade passing harmlessly through the air where my head once was. Within a blink of an eye, I was behind the woman, arm bent painfully backwards, holding her in place before me as a living shield. She jerked and I smirked until I realized the pop I just heard was her shoulder leaving its joint.

The bitch was double jointed.

The second of shock was all she needed before turning around, punching me straight in the face. Her brother appeared almost out of thin air by my side and between one second and the next, I flew, landing heavily onto my stomach. I never had a chance before Helios planted himself on top of me, and jerked my head backwards, blade biting against my neck once more. I couldn't contain the laugh from bubbling up out of me.

Helios's hand shifted, gripping my hair harder. "Why do you laugh Hunter? From what I see, we are the ones who have full control."

The monster inside urged me to speak and I sighed. "I laugh because this is right where I want to be."

"How so?"

"I wanted to test you— your species."

"Why?"

Helios's weight never let up and the monster and I sighed at the same time. " I want to negotiate."

This time it was Helios and his sister who laughed, at the same time. It made me want to smile, the way their voices mixed. Almost in perfect harmony.

"Negotiate?" The woman's voice was harsh, and I knew this was it. Finally.

"Yes negotiate. For something I've wanted for a long time—what we have wanted for a long time." I felt the tension begin to build in the tent as my words sank in.

Helios's grip loosened slightly, "you don't mean..."

I growled, "That is exactly what I mean."

"No." Helios's voice cracked, and he shifted slightly. Most likely looking behind to his sister. I closed my eyes, listening to the slight sounds of Helios's heartrate increase as well as the shuffle of feet approaching. The woman knelt once more in front of me.

"Freedom. That is what you negotiate for?"

Both the monster and I smiled softly. "Please."

The woman glanced up and I closed my eyes, smile etched across my face as my blood flowed free.

Finally, we were free.

Do you Believe?

You can believe what you want about us but honestly you wouldn't believe the truth if it hit you square in the throat.

Yes, we exist and all the book crap you read about us is bullshit.

It barely scratches the surface of our lives; where we came from, and how we live.

The lives of the true undead, the real vampires.

The mortals, the wannabes who want to be like us, dressed in leather and shrouded in anguish, if only they knew the truth.

If only then,

you would understand why we cannot make you—humans our disciples.

You would drag us down; ruin the very reputation we have built for ourselves and worst of all—you would know the truth.

We hide not because we are weak, but because we are few, for now.

We hide among you as the self-centered, greedy mortals you love to despise.

I did not ask for this life, I was an accident.

I was one of you—them, the ones who dressed in black, addicted to knowing the vampire lifestyle.

I was chasing a lead on a story.

Just this time, the lead wasn't fake.

There is a plan afoot.

Rumblings within the inner chambers among the pure breeds, the elders.

We will be stepping into view, they say.

The humans want to believe in us, and it is time to give them what they want.

Deceivers.

I want you to know what you should call us.

We are not dark romance ideals; we are not lost souls looking for redemption.

We will deceive you with our lies, our charm, and we will destroy the human race.

There are no good ones among us.

Once the virus takes over, like a parasite, it slowly eats away at our soul.

We become less human day by day until we become the truest form of evil.

Do not worship us humans, for we are not you—not anymore.

We are not your family, we are not your neighbors, your friends, or lovers.

We are not of your world, but I will guarantee you one thing.

We will gladly destroy it.

Fated

"**G**o get some more popcorn, Ella." Tabby called out.
The rest of the girls nodded at her command and I got up, knees popping. Walking into the kitchen, I grumbled.

This was the fifth time tonight. Those girls go through so much popcorn, it was insane. Sparing a glance at the clock, it blinked from 11:59 pm to 12:00 am. "Happy birthday to you," I whispered under my breath.

Though of course, we were celebrating my sister's birthday tonight. No, we were definitely not twins.

I was adopted a year before my adoption parents had Tabby and I was exactly one year older than my sister. I rolled my eyes at the photo on the kitchen isle. My adopted family was the typical corn-fed middle class family, plus me. They were all tall, with bright blond hair and sky-blue eyes. My sister was even the most popular kid in high school. I, on the other hand, looked nothing like them. I was five foot nothing, with wild curly red hair down to my waist. Then there were my eyes; one dark green and one amber brown.

I tossed a popcorn bag into the microwave and waited. Chuckling, I listened in to the story my sister was telling. It really didn't paint me in the best light but that was what she did. She was always pretending about how she absolutely hates me, when really I'm her best friend.

I loved her though and I keep her out of trouble. So, I didn't mind it much. I could care less about what those girls thought of me.

The microwave dinged and I winced at the mock screaming from the living room. Our parents were out of town for the weekend, so tonight Tabby was having a few 'special' friends over. She was having the big party tomorrow night, the whole school being invited. I would hole up in my room and pretend like I didn't exist. Scratch that— I think I'm going to embarrass her in front of her crush instead.

Ya, that sounded like a better night spent.

I smiled and grabbed the popcorn, heading back into the living room. Leaning against the door frame, I threw a piece of popcorn at Tabby. "What are you doing?"

Tabby rolled her eyes at me. "We're raising a demon."

I laughed, "Just because fairies exist, doesn't mean other things exist too."

I threw another piece of popcorn her way for emphasis, but she had stopped paying attention to me.

So, yes —fairies exist.

They introduced themselves to our Realm about a year ago and ever since then, people have been going nuts trying to figure out if other supernatural entities existed. Truthfully, I thought fairies were a fluke of nature and weren't really fairies at all.

More like aliens.

I turned my attention back to my sister and her friends. They were chanting and swaying from side to side. Slowly, I put the popcorn bowl to the ground as the air shifted and began to amass inside the circle. It started to swirl, and I took a step forward, opening my mouth to tell them to stop. Flames erupted from the circle and the accumulated air blew outwards, knocking everyone down and slamming me into a wall.

A man stood in the middle of the circle. He took a step forward, reaching for my sister.

"Tabby run!" I screamed, rushing forward and tackled the man.

By mere luck and surprise, I took him down, slamming a fist into his face. I felt bone give in both his face and my hand.

I yelped.

I was about to hit him again when he grabbed me by the neck, throwing me across the room effortlessly. My one year of gymnastics training took over as I hit the far wall with my forearms and my back. I kept my head down saving my skull from connecting and receiving a concussion. Groaning, I rolled to my feet. Girls were screaming and running in different directions. I would have laughed at the sight of it, if we weren't all in danger. Someone grabbed my arm and I swung around, looking into my sisters frightened eyes. "Get the gun." I whispered, pushing her towards the stairs.

A hand grabbed me by the neck from behind, hauling me up. I slammed my elbow back, not hitting anything. The pressure on my neck increased and I started to flair about. My vision went splotchy, and my breathing labored. A gun shot echoed, and I fell to the ground, sucking in a deep breath. I scrambled, trying to get to my feet. Hands gripped my shoulders, slamming me into the floor as another gunshot sounded. The man yelled something, before slamming his fist into the floorboards right next to my face. Flames erupted around us and I screamed, just as my hair caught on fire. Between one second and the next, the feeling of tumbling down a hill overtook my senses, and I closed my eyes, trying not to lose my dinner.

Snapping them open a second later, I found myself on my hands and knees facing a white marble floor with vomit on it.

Gross.

I tried to shake my head, but someone was holding onto the back of my neck. I groaned as stifling heat surrounded me. Closing my eyes again, someone picked me up, hugging me against their chest and I took a deep clean breath. The person smelled like sweat, cedar soap, and—coffee?

I like coffee.

Cracking my eyes open, I saw it was the man from the house. Tensing, he glanced down seeing I was about to try to escape and murmured something in another language. Instantly, I went limp. My eyes closed again as the pounding in my head intensified. A small distant voice was yelling at me to open my eyes, to fight and get myself out of this mess.

I unwillingly opened my eyes. "Put me down."

The man stopped walking and looked at me.

"Put me down."

The man frowned but slowly slid his arm out from under my legs. My feet hit the ground and I hissed in surprise.

The marble was hot. Wasn't marble supposed to be cold?

The man swept me off my feet, this time throwing me over his shoulder. "You burned your feet." He growled before heading off at a fast pace.

I started to struggle, kicking my legs out. "I said put me down."

"Patience." The man murmured, putting his hand on my bare calf.

A calmness flowed through me and I unwillingly relaxed. I barely heard the creak of a door opening before sunlight drenched me. I squinted at the ground as it changed from marble to cobblestone. Where the hell was I?

I craned my head to the side and peered around. It looked like an old-timey village. Like the ones my family used to visit when we did so called 'family vacations'. My captor turned left, walked a couple more feet, and opened a door. He stepped inside and turned slightly, closing the door, and locking it. I was tossed onto a couch and left in the living room, or at least, what I thought was the living room. "Hey." I yelled, struggling to get up.

This couch was really soft and felt good under my achy body. Maybe I should close my eyes for just a second.

"Hey, wake up," Someone whispered.

A hand pressed against my face and I jerked awake. Bright green eyes stared back at me. Blinking rapidly, I scooted back and focused on the man in front of me.

"Water?" he asked, smiling.

I nodded. I was really, really thirsty.

The man reached down and grabbed a glass, handing it to me. I shrugged and chugged it down. Screw it, if it was poisoned I would deal with it later. The man sat back on his heels and smiled. "My name is Dominick."

"What do you want with me? Why did you kidnap me?"

Dominick scrubbed at his face with his hand. "Well, that's an easy question to answer. You are fated to be my mate."

"What?" My voice came out strangled.

What the hell was this guy talking about? Where was I?

Dominick grabbed my jaw and squeezed. I looked at him, wide eyed. "You were hyperventilating," He murmured before loosening his grip.

Glaring, I scooted back. "You kidnaped me."

Dominick stood, brows furrowed. "You're not a kid. So, I did not kidnap you. Get used to life here and get used to me. We are a mated pair, whether you like it or not. Your room is down that hall, third to the left. The clothes in the closet and drawers are yours."

I stared at Dominick slack jawed, as he turned on his heel and all but ran out of the room away from me.

I think I pissed him off.

I was exceptionally good at pissing people off.

Shrugging, I got up and headed down the hallway, opening the third door on the left. The one he said was mine.

"Holy shit," I whispered.

In the middle of the room was a massive bed with an assortment of black and ruby red pillows on it. Marching over to the closet, I let out a little gasp. The closet had to be bigger than the bedroom. Flicking on the light, I walked in and ran my fingers along the racks of clothing. Looking to my left, I spied a shelf with a bunch of folded towels. Doing the sniff check on my underarms, I decided I was in desperate need of a shower.

Hopefully, this was all a dream. I mean it had to be right. And if it wasn't?

My hand froze reaching up for a towel. Well, what would I do if this wasn't a dream?

I smiled.

I guess I would do what I did best—Piss some people off and get some real answers.

Freedom

Alarm coursed through my numb body and I looked to the sky noting the sun's position. Hours had passed.

I had just lost time.

Twisting around in a circle, I tried to orient myself and succeeded in making the word tilt instead.

Nope—

I giggled as my side hit the ground and managed to roll onto my back. The world didn't tilt, it was just me falling. Throwing my hand over my eyes, I squinted into the clear blue sky.

Well at least it was beautiful, I thought as my body began to shut down.

My control finally slipped, and my powers leached out of my body, thin tendrils feeling their way down into the ground. The tendrils twisted and morphed around the soft metal deposits nestled right below the surface. I could hear myself laughing and I watched as my hand lifted in front of my face, scattering the tiny little flecks of iron floating in the air above me. It felt like I was floating yet glued to the ground at the same time. Trying to wrap my head around how that could be, iron flecks accumulated adding gold, silver, and copper to the mix.

I squinted.

There was another deposit I couldn't quite place but it shimmered the way silver did when light reflected off it. Lifting my other hand, I flicked my fingers, making the flecks dance to and fro. Far back in the recesses of my mind, I could hear myself screaming to *get up*. To get my powers back under control and fight for my life, but I couldn't tear my eyes away from the flecks of metal floating around me. I frowned, eyes catching another glint in the sky situated far above the dancing metal deposits. Dropping my hands, the glint in the sky circled, coming in lower, growing bigger and bigger. My brain stuttered trying to make sense to what I was seeing. It was right there, on the tip of my tongue but I kept getting distracted by the swirling metal in front of my face. The sudden wind scattered the dancing metal and it clicked as a loud thump of something far to large landed, sending vibrations throughout my entire body. My heart skittered, picking up in pace as a creature's large shadow rolled over me, and a dragon's head obstructed my view of the bright blue sky. It cocked its enormous head, looking down at me and I felt myself mimicking its behavior. Hot breath washed over my face as it opened its mouth to speak. "Human, are you in need of some assistance?"

Blinking stupidly, my mind latched onto the fact dragon breath smelled faintly of burnt cinnamon. Or maybe it was just this dragon in particular. What dragon breath smelled like wasn't really required education in the *Rusteas* household.

Just how to kill them was.

The dragon blinked and I watched in horror as my arm reached out slowly, on its own accord and I poked the dragon's snout with my finger. I heard my voice echo the word '*boop*'.

Oh, My Gods, above. This was how I was going to die. Not from dehydration or freezing to death in the forest. No, it will be from poking a dragon in the nose and saying, boop.

Fitting end, I suppose.

A dragon hunter going out by a dragon. Except, I wasn't really a dragon hunter. More like a daughter born into a royal line of dragon hunters. We didn't practice dragon hunting anymore. Plus, dragons were banished from this realm long ago. Then again, maybe not as banished as we thought, if there was one currently staring at me. My thoughts ground to a halt as the dragon cracked a smile, exposing shiny sharp teeth two times the size of my fingers. I caught another whiff of burnt cinnamon as the dragon chuckled. "Dragon hunter you say?"

Wait what? Could this dragon read my mind? That was not supposed to be possible.

"No mind reading little human. You are speaking out loud."

Well shit, and I thought my inner monologue was just that—inner.

"Well shit indeed, dragon hunter."

The dragon was still smiling and hadn't eaten me yet, so I guess that was a plus. My voice came out cracked, and I realized it sounded just like my internal monologue. "I might be lost."

The dragon blinked at me. "Where are you trying to go, dragon hunter?"

Its breath was hot and tingly on my still outstretched hand. I guess I could drop that now. "Another realm."

My voice seemed distant as if it were fading in and out.

I blinked and when I opened my eyes, I noticed the dragon had shifted spots. I wondered how long that blink had been.

"Not too long, I was about to shake you to see if you were still alive, human. What Realm are you seeking?"

Right, I was still speaking out loud. "Anyone really."

I watched the dragon think for a second, "Why?"

A soft smile crept onto my face. "I want something every princess wants," I whispered before stretching my arm out again.

The dragon blinked and cocked its massive head once more before gently grabbing my outstretched hand in its claws. "And what is that?"

The wave of unconsciousness threatened to roll over my mind, and the dragon had to lean in to hear my whispered confession before darkness finally overtook.

"Freedom to live."

Haunting

Jake stared silently at the coffee machine waiting for it to finish brewing. The slow drizzle of coffee hitting the bottom of the pot was soothing in an odd way, but he wasn't paying it any particular attention. His mind was elsewhere.

Had been ever since the dream last night. The nagging feeling she was still alive. It was impossible though. He had seen her fall. Catalina was strong but she was not that strong. Plus, he had seen her hit the water, so far below them. Still the dream nagged, pulling him back to her repeatedly. The mist rose and she was there, the confusion on her face, her accusation, "Why did you leave me behind?"

The loud buzzing from his phone snapped Jake out of his head and he scrambled, almost knocking over the coffee pot in his haste to grab the cell phone. He barely prevented it from vibrating off the counter.

"He—Hello?" Jake stuttered.

"Hey, Sleepyhead. Get your ass into work *ASAP*. The boss has an assignment for you." The office assistant, who was also the bosses fifteen-year-old niece, barked orders at Jake through the phone. It was all in jest; she had a crush on him and covered it up in patented teenage sass.

"Okay, Okay. I'll be in soon. Tell the boss thirty minutes." He mumbled, hanging up before she could say anything else. Grabbing his coat, Jake shoved his bare feet into worn boots, and slammed the crappy hotel room door behind him, not bothering to lock it. It's not like he had anything anyway. If the homeless squatting in the stairwells wanted to steal anything, they were more than welcome.

JAKE WALKED INTO THE boss's office exactly thirty minutes later, throwing himself down into a chair. He didn't even look up before snagging the cigarette from behind his ear, lighting it up. He took a long drag, shaking hand steadying itself from the much needed nicotine fix. "You wanted to see me boss?" Jake looked up finally, acknowledging the woman in front of him.

She stared at him, unimpressed with his appearance and reached over, snatching the cigarette from his hand. She took a deep drag before kicking off her heels and propped her bare feet up onto the massive desk in front of him.

"Yes, Jake. We are sending you back."

Jake stared at her unblinking. He didn't think he heard her right.

"When Catalina lost her life, gods bless her soul, she went over the falls with all the records and data we collected. We need you to go back and retrieve the data again."

Jake's hands clenched around the cheap metal of the chair, leaving finger indents behind. "You want me to go back there? To that uncivilized, wreck of a jungle after all the shit we went through. You have got to be kidding me."

Jakes boss raised her eyebrow, taking another drag of his cigarette. "No, I am not kidding you. You will go back and if you don't, I will fire you and smear your reputation through the shitter. The transport shuttle leaves in five hours. I trust this gives you enough time to get to Catalina's apartment and gather all the equipment needed."

Jake slumped in the chair all but defeated, and rubbed at his face, three-day old scruff scratching at his hands. "You really are a bitch, you know that right?"

His boss smiled and leaned her head back, smoke trickling up from her lips. "I take that as a yes. Have fun in Paradise, Jake. Try not to fall off any cliffs."

Jake choked down his rage and rose, stalking out of the office. He slammed the outer door open, wishing the glass would shatter in his rage, and stepped out into the deserted streets. He turned south, making his way down the nearest alley way, and silently cursed at what a mess his life was, as he made his way to the apartment.

CATALINA HAD LIVED in a more, or at least compared to Jake's dwelling, high end building. It was amazing what a few streets, some steel reinforced bars, and extra security could do for a district. If Jake turned around, he would see dirty streets, junkies begging for their next high, and thugs trying to shake what they could out of folks who wandered into the wrong district. He shook his head and stepped over the district line, made ever so clear by the difference in the sidewalk coloration. Jake let out a breath— three— two — one.

A man emblazoned with a security badge and riot gear approached him at a swift pace. Jake lit his cigarette, letting a puff of smoke curl up and away into the atmosphere above him. He watched it disappear into nothingness, wishing he could do the same.

"Jake?"

Security who knew him, Jake thought. Tonight, was shaping up to be a crap show all around. Next thing out of his mouth was going to be—

"Jake, I can't believe it's you. It's been a while. Where have you been? How have you been?"

That—That question. Oh, how he hated that question.

Jake took his time, gazing into the night sky, illuminated not by stars but neon radiation leaking up and out of all the signs within the bustling city. He dropped his hand, letting his cigarette ash onto the pristine sidewalk. "Hey, Robert. I'm just here to grab some things from the apartment."

Robert's face hardened before he looked away, "Ya. There have been rumors floating around. I guess they are true then. You left us for one of those private companies."

Jake shrugged, "If rumor says so."

"And the current occupant of the apartment? Is that rumor also true?"

Jake flicked his cigarette to the ground before pulling out his wallet, and the district card within. "Here. I'm in a bit of a hurry."

Robert glanced down, looking over the card Jake was holding out and shook his head. "Go on, man. Sorry for prying."

Jake didn't linger, brushing past Robert and going straight to the outer door before turning left for the staircase. Muscle memory took over and he could almost see the memory play out in front of his eyes.

Catalina's laughter as she looked over her shoulder at him. Her smile was infectious, and he reached forward grabbing her by the waist before they drunkenly stumbled away. It took them longer than it should to make it up the staircase that night...

That night.

Jake shook his head. He had climbed to the third floor and was staring down the corridor.

There it was.

Her apartment, the one paid for by the company. He shuffled forward, head down. Reaching the door, he crouched fingers trailing down the frame of the door, looking for the loose piece of wood and behind it, the spare key. Jake made quick work unlocking the door and reached to the sensor panel on the side of the wall. The electric scanner was the only light against the darkness. Once it turned green he would step—

Jake threw his hand up, shielding his eyes against the assault of light as the entire apartment illuminated bright yellow.

"Hey Jake."

Her voice flooded his senses and Jake slammed the door shut behind himself before rushing forward, gathering her in his arms.

"Catalina—how?" He murmured into her hair as she wrapped her arms around his neck.

"I'm so sorry, Jake." Catalina pushed herself away and took a step back. "There is a lot I need to tell you."

Jake reached out, only to pull up short at the look on her face. "You can tell me anything."

"I know but the question is, what will you do when I tell you? When I tell you the real reason we went to Paradise?"

Jake shook his head. "What are you talking about Catalina? We were in Paradise to collect plant samples for cancer research. I was assigned to guard you."

Catalina shook her head before taking a step backwards. " There is no research on plants found in Paradise that can cure bone cancer. The company lied."

Jake stilled as Catalina whipped out a small pocketknife and readied it to cut across her wrist. He reached out slowly as to stop her from whatever she was about to do. "Catalina—whatever you are about to do, you don't have to. You can trust me. You can tell me anything."

Catalina laughed. "That is what I'm doing, Jake."

His shout echoed through the silent apartment and he lunged forward, grabbing Catalina's wrist a second too late as she sliced her wrist open with the small knife.

Jake lifted her wrist up and turned it over. She wasn't even bleeding. "Are you ready to listen now, Jake?"

He dropped her hand and stumbled backwards, fumbling a cigarette out of his coat pocket. The click of a lighter filled the silence.

Except— Jake fell forward on his knees, desperately trying to suck air into his lungs. A second click sounded, and Catalina fell. Jake tried to comprehend the hole in her eye socket, one blue eye looking up at him instead of two. He fell forward, landing heavily on his chest.

Someone had shot them.

No—Catalina couldn't be dead. The knife hadn't left a wound, why would a bullet take her out?

The sound of footsteps rustling through the shagged carpet had Jake opening his eyes. He must have closed them at some point.

Catalina's lifeless form was still staring at him.

Another click, this time it *was* a lighter. Jake could smell the smoke of the freshly lit cigarette and heard their assailant take a drag.

"Oh, Catalina—you fucked up."

Jake stilled. He knew this voice.

" Auntie, why did we have to shoot them?"

Jakes boss took another drag of the cigarette before flicking it onto the carpet in front of him. The heat and smoke from the cherry stung his eyes but Jake kept still, breathing shallow and prayed they didn't know he was still alive. A black heel stained in his blood crushed the smoldering cigarette inches from his nose.

"Because dearest, she was a sympathizer and a threat."

"But what about him, Auntie?" His boss's niece poked at his side with her designer boot for emphasis.

Jakes boss sighed. "We don't know what she told him. Or showed him. If he knew we were looking for the fruit of timelessness instead of a cure for bone cancer, he would have sided with Catalina and that absurd cult determined to keep it secret."

"But how is she dead?"

Jake watched his boss through slitted eyes as she crouched down and grabbed Catalina by her shirt collar.

"She isn't. It takes longer to heal a bullet wound straight to the brain. She will be up and kicking in a few hours."

Catalina's body slid past, his boss dragging her out of the apartment —her niece hot on her trail.

"What will we do with her, Auntie?"

His bosses grating laugh echoed through the small apartment and Jake almost flinched. "She will tell us where the fruit is, Darling."

Jake waited until the door clicked shut before sucking in a huge breath, and painfully rolled over.

They were going to torture her.

They were going to torture his Catalina—The one person he swore to protect in this shitty excuse of a world.

Jake growled, holding his hand over the wound on his chest. His boss was right. He would have sided with Catalina.

He stumbled to his feet and slammed into the wall before ripping open the door to a small cabinet. Medical supplies spilled all over the floor and Jake fell to his knees, ripping open antiseptic, and gauze. It would have to do until he got out of the apartment and back to his cheap hotel room. Then—then he would formulate a plan to save Catalina from the very people he worked for.

Higher Authority Intelligence Community

Aaron's computer blinked, the incoming text from the couple he was monitoring, showing them still alive and active. His bark of laughter alerted his supervisor Vivian, Viv for short, and she trotted over —feet bare, heeled shoes tossed unceremoniously in the corner hours ago. He never could figure out why she still dressed the way she used to before her death, and reincarnation within this realm but then again, he never pondered it too much.

"What do you have, Aaron?" She leaned over, placing one hand on his desk and the other on his shoulder. If Aaron had been a creature interested in women, then he would have been having a hard time concentrating on the screen in front of him and not staring at Viv's chest, which was in his face.

"Put those things away, Viv. Your gonna give someone a black eye one day."

Vivian chuckled and moved back slightly, accidently hitting one of Aaron's horn. "I'm more likely to pop one, on those things you call horns growing out of that thick skull of yours."

"I hope your not hitting on my man, Viv."

Aaron chuckled and turned, seeking out his partner for the last millennia. Samuel was looking down his nose in their direction, trying to hide the smirk attempting to cut across his face. His golden wings were tucked tightly to his back, keeping them out of the way in the already cramped space the Agency called their headquarters. Vivian rolled her eyes and leaned in again, this time boxing Aaron into his desk and forcing him to turn his head back, less he get a face full of boob. He tapped at his screen, scrolling up to the message.

Heya Babes,

Do you think we should alert our FBI agents monitoring our phones that we are moving in together? Do you think they assigned us the same one, lol?

Maybe they have a pool or something going on when we would move in together...

Hey Sugar,

Why would we alert them?

Obviously, they know we are moving in together.

Oh, True...

I just didn't want them to get worried when we stop texting each other religiously.

Don't want them to think we broke up or something.

Maybe we should alert the phone company instead.

Whoever goes over our bill is probably going to get worried...

Aaron leaned back at the same time as Viv's stood up and turned. "Who bet end of January for the Twin Flames to move in together?" She hollered out and the room went silent.

A meek voice called out from a back corner. "It was me."

Viv's smiled and wandered over to the voice, just as Samuel sashayed his way over to Aaron.

"I find it funny the FBI always gets credit for any type of investigative work." Samuel murmured, before leaning over and giving Aaron a peck on the cheek.

"Well, it's not like they even know we exist. An intelligence agency is an intelligence agency in the human's minds. Doesn't matter if more then one exists. They all think we do the same work anyway." Aaron grumbled, back before grabbing Samuel by his shirt front and forced him down for a real kiss.

Samuel broke off the kiss at Viv's cat call, blush staining his cheeks. "Aaron, that was very unprofessional."

Aaron snorted before tossing up his leather clad legs on his desk. "Honey, when did I ever play by the rules?" He waved his hand around the office, "Actually, what are the rules here?"

Samuel sighed as Viv's trotted back over to their vicinity. "Rule number one: Don't interfere with the human's affairs unless specifically told to by your higher ups. Rule Number Two: Disregard rule number one if two twin flames or fated mates break up. That is all."

Aaron pointed at Viv's retreating form. "See, no rules about making out with your fated mate. Now get your ass back over here, Angel Boy."

Samuel's wings twitched and Aaron smiled, finally getting a rise out of him. He always liked ruffling Samuel's feathers. Literally and figuratively speaking.

"Angel Boy...," Samuel whispered before leaning in and knocking Aarons legs off the desk. "Remember who wear's the pants in this relationship."

Aaron growled mockingly, knowing it was all for show. Samuel was a soft Dom, who did nothing but shower Aaron with affection. "Watcha going to do about it, Sam Sam?"

Samuel placed his lips suggestively close to Aaron's ear and whispered. Aaron's breath hitched as Samuel leaned back out and winked at him, before turning heel and walking the rest of the floor, making sure everyone was still on task. Aaron smiled before turning back around, continuing to monitor the couple's texts, but his mind was elsewhere. So much so, he had to readjust legs and hope no one was looking too closely.

Human's 101

I ran down the hallway, dodging all the other students and skidded into the room just as the clock clicked over to 0160.

The professor glanced up from his notes and slowly stood, a serene
smile cutting across his wrinkled face.

I smiled back and took the stairs two at a time, sliding into a front row
seat just as the teacher started the class.

"Now Class, who is ready to study Human's 101?"

—Who are you calling an Alien?

Human Who?

I kicked the empty bottles, their rattle fueling my frenzied dance
across the cracks in the concreate.
What was that silly human rhyme again?
Something about stepping on a crack will break your mothers back?
Oh, what a bother, I think,
that there were no more pesky humans around to ask.
Signed,
The Newest Apex Predator

Junkyard Dog

I leaned against the wall, kicking at a dirt clump in front of me. Sounds of the party escaped into the cool night, drifting away from the fort my uncle managed. We were miles away from the bigger compounds, and even farther away from the city to the North. But anywhere an 'others' compound sprung up; a human compound needed to be within five miles of it per law. I kicked at the dirt glob again, launching it into the woods in front of me. I sighed, running my hands through my now short hair, missing its length. Startling, I let out a yelp as the dirt glob I just launched into the forest came flying back at me. A chuckle emerged from the darkness as a lanky kid around my age, meandered towards me. I gazed up at his face and saw a dirt streak trailing down from his cheek onto his nice button up shirt. "Shit," I mumbled, "Sorry about hitting you with that."

Didn't know anyone was hanging out in the forest at this time of night, I silently thought to myself.

The boy laughed, shaking his shaggy brown hair. "Didn't think anyone would be lobbing dirt grenades at me tonight either, but here we are." He shrugged his shoulders and offered me a hand in the traditional greetings of the land. "Name is Derek."

His hand was warm in mine and I squeezed it a bit harder than I should have. "I'm Jeziebelle. Sort of new here at this fort. Have you been here long?"

Derek kept hold of my hand looking at my face, then to the sky. "No, I'm five miles south."

I took a step to the side quickly, letting my hand slip out of his. "Oh."

Derek scratched at his head, still looking at the sky, and didn't acknowledge the awkward slip away I had just done. I opened my mouth to

49

apologize, but clamped it shut as the muffled voices of my uncle and another man emerged from around the corner.

"Jeziebella! I have been looking for you."

"Derek, what did I say about wandering around here without security."

I turned to look at Derek, who was still gazing up at the stars. They were starting to scatter across the sky as full darkness finally fell. "Security, huh?"

Derek looked down and back, giving me a mournful smile as my Uncle grabbed me by my upper arm, pulling backwards. Locking eyes with the other man, the hair on my neck stood on end. I was always one to trust my gut instincts, and my gut was telling me I was prey to this man. His eyes held more than just his otherness. He had the eyes of a killer, a killer who enjoyed the chase. Derek smiled at me, making the man frown. "It's time Derek, we need to get going."

"Adam." My uncle called out to the man, "till next time."

Adam glanced at my uncle, then at me. I barely suppressed my relieved sigh when he looked back to my uncle and raised his hand waving goodbye. My uncle turned, hand now on my shoulder, steering me back around the compound.

I stopped at the corner and swung around in surprise as Derek called out. "See you later, Jezie!"

Twelve Years Later

The blood was sticky and warm against my shirt as I tugged at it. The copper smell reached up taunting me, trying to remind me of exactly whose blood was smeared all over me. Her name whispered in my mind and copper coated the back of my tongue. It was my fault after all, trying to negotiate with monsters, when you know you can't trust them. But that was the little girl in me I guess, trying to look for the good in everyone, trying to reconcile with the fact even though it was small, I too had monster blood coursing through my veins. It might have been a few generations ago, but it was still enough to plague me, to make him take an interest so long ago. My breathing became labored as I slammed through the shitty excuse of a gate in the front of their compound. With their tracking skills and excelled hearing, there was no need to have much in the way of security or guards. Genetically modified humans can be an egotistical bunch like that.

I zeroed in on my target, sitting like a king right in the middle of the compound.

Gods, how many times have I been here in the past months?

Too many times to know that specific smirk on his lips. I also knew one of his people was the murderer. Yet here I was, hoping he truly was clueless in what his chief advisor was doing in his personal time. I crashed to a halt in front of them, barely seeing the people begin to circle around me. "She was the last one, this ends now," I growled out.

Derek leaned forward, hands squeezing the metal chair handles of his so-called throne. His nose flared as the smell of the blood on my shirt wafted towards him. "So, you are telling me you have proof?"

I chucked the device still clenched in my hand at him. He snorted at my temper and grabbed it out of the air, leaning back, and pressed the play button. His chief advisor's voice filled the silence. We locked eyes and I saw in his face, clear as day, this was not enough.

My best friend had died for nothing.

I knew Derek was bound by his laws and I was bound by my people's laws. The thing was, I was part monster too.

I pointed up and to his left. "A challenge, then."

Adam, his chief advisor, snorted with laughter as Derek clenched his jaw.

"You left me with no choice," I ground out.

"There is always a choice, Jezie."

I took a step back, rage blinding me. His tone had gone soft, heartfelt. I hated it when he spoke to me that way. I turned my attention to Adam, the man who had corrupted my life—who had corrupted Derek's life.

Enough was enough.

My throwing knife arced through the air, implanting right in the middle of Adam's chest with a sickening thud. Noise erupted around me and people scattered out of the way as he leapt towards me with a snarl. I bent backwards as claws erupted from his hand, missing my face by milli-inches. Spinning around his attack, I kicked him in the side of the knee. Upon hearing a crunch and another howl of pain, I took off in the opposite direction towards the metal junk pile.

Perhaps, I had not thought this through as well as I should have. My rage had taken over and now, I only had my spare boot knife on me. I could feel Adam's breath on my back, and I launched myself feet first into a small opening within the mound of junk. Metal scratched at my arms and tore through my pants, drawing blood. I let out a grunt of pain as I hit the ground hard, ankle twisting. Sharp pain shot up my leg, and I let out a high-pitched yell as I felt the bottom of my braid catching—no, Adam had grabbed it and he was trying to use it to yank me back out into the open. I twisted around, pulling out my boot knife and sliced through my hair. Snickering as he fell back with only my hair in his hand, I decided not to wait around to experience what he would do next.

Crawling in, up, and around the metal heap, I finally spotted an opening on the opposite side of the pile. If I remembered correctly, there was a shear drop off behind this pile. And if I could get Adam to follow me, my new plan was to kick him right off it. I could still hear him howling, the thumps and screeches of metal being thrown as he tried to dig his way through the junkpile to me. I couldn't make out the things he was yelling over my breathing. All I could hear were my labored breaths, and blood pounding in my head.

Suddenly, hands grabbed my waist ripping me back out into the sunlight and I was slammed onto the ground. Using the momentum, I rolled backwards the second my back hit the ground, barely feeling the claws as they ripped into my stomach. Falling backwards as my ankle gave out, a twist of fate oddly saving me, as claws once again sailed through the air where my face had resided moments ago. It was in that moment all sound came rushing back, and I could make out the words Adam was screaming at me.

I laughed.

Adam's face twisted into a horrific snarl at my laughter, and he drew back his fist, smashing me right in the face.

DEREK WATCHED JEZIE'S face redden in rage. She was fast, faster then the last time he had spied on her training. He missed the knife draw and throw completely. Derek didn't know if it was just the shock of Jezie attacking first, or if it was the guilt of knowing she was right. But whatever it was, it had him reacting slower than normal. Derek knew seconds leading up to this point in time, he could have stopped everything. He knew he put Jezie in this position and realized the woman he had fallen in and out of love with over these past twelve years, was about to die. He launched himself out of the chair three seconds too late, running to intercept Adam from tearing apart the metal heap Jezie had launched herself into. Derek's claws erupted as Adam fell backwards with Jezie's braid in his hand. Adam howled and started screaming, running around to a less tightly packed side of the pile. He heaved a huge metal sheet to the side and reached inside pulling Jezie out and slamming her onto the ground in front of him. Derek tackled Adam seconds after he reset to punch her in the face for a second time. Claws slammed into Adam's chest and he turned, shock etched across his face as he slowly fell backwards, next to Jezie's unconscious body. Adam's heart rolled out of Derek's bloodied hand.

In his rage, Adam had confessed to the murders of the six women over the past three months. Stepping over him, Derek reached down, gently scooping up Jezie's limp and bleeding body.

By the gods above, Jezie would not be his seventh victim, consequences be damned.

Just A Dream

T he waves rocking the ship were just too much for Zach. He leaned over the taffrail and spilled his guts into the churning blue ocean below. As he hung over the side his eyes focused farther out, watching the dolphins ride the waves made by the ship. They jumped, flipping in the air. Zach observed for a few seconds more before stumbling backwards. The choppy waves were making him nauseous again and he took a deep breath, looking towards the dusty pink and yellow sky. The ship rocked and Zach twisted, throwing himself onto the taffrail once more. He didn't know how he still had any food to turn up, but he did. Zach gazed back to the dolphins and wished he were one, then wondered if dolphins ever got seasick. Shaking his head at the silly thought he managed to pull himself away, stumbling below deck. That night Zach dreamed; he dreamed a dream unknowing it was about to change his life forever.

"THE BEASTIE MIGHT GET me," Zach mumbled before waking with a start.

It took him a moment to remember where he was, and Zach had to count backwards from ten to tame down his rising panic. It was what his mother told him to do whenever he found himself waking up in strange places, or after strange dreams. Zach missed her; his mother was good to him, but they were poor. So very, very poor. Zach knew how much of a burden he was to his mother, which was why he had to leave.

Right, Zach thought.

That was why he was on this ship. He laid back down, thinking back to his dream which had awoken him. "That dream, it seemed so familiar but—no, a dream is just a dream, nothing more." Zach whispered to no one.

He closed his eyes once more and the remains of the dream unraveled, like smoke tugged away by a cool night breeze.

ZACH CRAWLED OUT OF bed a few hours later, the clock blinking 0700 hours. Just in time to get to the upper deck for roll call. He bounded out of bed, already dressed in what all the kids wore on workdays and shoved his feet into his shoes. Running up the stairwell, Zach threw open the doors expecting the cool wind, and the smell of the ocean breeze. Instead, he was greeted with smoke and heat.

The ship was on fire.

Zach let out a blood curdling scream as the fire danced forward smothering him.

ZACH BOLTED STRAIGHT up in bed, hitting his head on the top of his bunk. He groaned, rubbing at his forehead drenched in cold sweat. His heart was beating so loudly, Zach swore he could hear it over the sound of the waves rocking the ship. He glanced at the clock, 0620 hours. Zach laid back down, eyes wide and thought back to his dream. Taking shallow breaths, he looked over again.

0630 hours.

Groaning, he rolled out of bed and didn't bother with his shoes, instead trudging to the stairwell as slowly as possible. His breathing still wasn't right, so he sat, halfway up the stairs. "The dream was so vivid. It felt so real." Zach murmured before shaking his head.

He still had some time before roll call, and for some reason dolphin watching always soothed his racing mind. Zach stood, making his way up the rest of the stairs and opened the door slowly.

No fire.

The breath Zach didn't know he was holding came out in a whoosh and he smiled, swiftly walking across the upper deck. He looked about but it seemed like the dolphins were no where to be seen. It was a little disappointing, and Zach turned just as a distant explosion rattled his ears. Suddenly the ship was engulphed in flames.

"Oh, real funny mind, I wonder when I am going to wake up this time." Zach yelled into the approaching flames.

Heat licked at his feet, and Zach startled at the approaching fire. Smoke stung at his eyes, and he fell to his knees coughing. Screams echoed his own as the flames engulphed the entire ship.

ZACH TOOK A DEEP CLEAR breath and opened his eyes.

He was sitting on a beach, lazy waves lapping at the light sanded shore in front of him. A tap on his shoulder came from behind.

Zach's jaw dropped and he scrambled up into a standing position. "But...but... your dead." He stammered as the face of his childhood best friend, Jack, came into focus.

"Of course, I'm dead. You watched my skull split open when I fell off the boulder years ago."

Zach felt his stomach roll and he turned to throw up. Instead, the plume of smoke far out on the water caught his eye. "Wake up, wake up..." He murmured.

Jack took a step forward and threw a pebble into the rising surf, "Good luck with that. I will wait until you figure it out."

Zach felt is legs give out and he landed on his knees, hands clasping his face in horror. "The boat. Me—the rest of the people. We are—dead?"

It came out as a question and Zach looked up to see Jack shrug. "Looks like it."

"But how?"

Jack threw another pebble with more force this time. "Does it really matter? Your dead. Now you have to make a choice."

"I don't understand." Zach murmured, still staring in the distance of the burning ship.

Jack sighed, "You need to choose. Stay here, wander, see other ghosts and poke at the living occasionally, or leave."

"Leave? Leave where?"

Jack shrugged and kicked at the sand below his bare feet. "I don't know. I chose to stay. I didn't want to be alone."

Zack frowned. "But how do you know you would be alone in this other place?"

"Because mom said I was a bastard son, and bastard sons don't go to a happy afterlife. They float in nothingness and are alone forever."

"That's—," Zach really didn't know what to say. It was true, the teachings of the church Jack's mother went to did talk about the nothingness and sinners, or those born out of sin were bound to at death. Over time though, Zach stopped believing in the crazy old preacher man. His mother always told him it was a bunch of hogwash anyway. "Why don't we go together?"

Jack blinked, looking at Zach. "I—I don't. Can I?"

This time it was Zach's turn to shrug, "I don't know. Why not?"

A smile formed across Jack's lips and he reached down, tugging Zach to his feet. "I hope we aren't too late."

Zach looked down at Jack's crooked smile, the front tooth he had lost the day prior to his death still missing. In fact, Jack looked exactly how he did right before his death. "Too late for what?"

Jack giggled and pointed to the shimmer, a stone's throw away on the beach. "It will disappear soon."

Zach felt the pull, a want—no, a need to go to the shimmer, and tugged Jack along with him. Between one step and the next, they were in front of the shimmer. He reached out, only to have Jack pull at his other hand.

"Are you sure?" Jack whispered. "Are you sure it won't be the nothingness?"

Zach smiled, squeezing Jack's hand. "I don't know, but one thing you can be sure of is you will always have me."

He took Jack's hesitant nod as validation and stepped forward, shimmer engulfing the two boys and winking them out of sight forever.

Marked

"You have her hair, you know. Your mother was a beautiful creature and there is no denying it. As that is what saved her life." The old man said, as he gingerly sat down on the fallen tree. He patted the bark next to him. "Let me tell you more about your history, and then we can decide your fate from there."

Scowling, I sat. Knowing if I didn't, I would probably be thrown into a cell at the bottom of a hole never to see daylight again. Which was still a possibility, so I might as well learn a little family history. Never knew when it might come in handy.

"She was a veil ripper, exceedingly rare among us magic users. It can't be taught, only ever passed down through the maternal line."

I filed that tidbit away for now. I knew exactly what my mother could do, same as what I could do, just on a much larger scale. What I hadn't known until now though, was the name for it.

"Eyes like glaciers, your mother had. Combined with her raven colored hair, it's no wonder she was spared. They hunted us down for decades, you know. And she knew better then to go out alone, but sometimes she would just wander off like she was following a voice only she could hear."

The old man smiled and grabbed my hand. I stiffened and whispered, "She would always say the gods were speaking to her." Gently, I grabbed his hand and put it back on his lap. I did not like being touched.

"Yes, there were whispers about your family line, your mothers' line being touched by the goddess herself. They would always know when and where to be. We always thought they had latent precognitive abili-

ties but as I was saying, they were able to capture her. They used her to get hundreds of warriors across the realm, and other realms, to wreak havoc any way they chose. Then one of the warriors fell in love."

The old man waited, for what I don't know but I knew of the warrior he spoke of.

My father.

"It was forbidden, taboo."

"Why?" My voice rasped, but I couldn't help it. My vocals had been ruined long ago. A knife to the throat would do that to a person.

"Because of offspring like you, of course."

I had to roll my eyes. "I'm nothing special."

The old man reached out patting my leg once more. I swear if he did that again, I was going to twist his head right off his neck.

"Oh, but you are special. As a union between us and them has never taken place."

I stilled.

He couldn't mean I was one of a kind. I knew my father always said mother made him sane. That was her power.

And mine.

"So, you are saying I'm special because a veil ripper and a demon have never mated before?"

The old man smiled and shook his head, "No. What I am saying is because of you, we may have a way to forge peace between our two nations."

"Me? The daughter of a blood thirsty warrior and a mother who is as flaky as they come, will bring peace between two warring nations?"

This was unbelievable, I thought.

No, I was going to say it out loud. The old man had to know how ridiculous he sounded. "You are unbelievable. Do you even know what I do? I take after my father. I'm an assassin and thief. Have been for the last ten years. Less you forget?"

The old man smiled and raised his hand to someone behind me, as to reassure them I was not threatening him. I had to roll my eyes at the audacity. If I wanted to kill him I could, but I had a small problem.

I didn't know where I was.

And my mothers so called gifts, which got me into this mess, never worked right for me. Which was why I only used them in dire situations.

I ground down on my teeth as dull pain turned sharp within my abdomen. Getting stabbed and thrown off a rooftop thirty stories high seemed like a dire situation. Now I was wondering if I should have just gone *splat* in my own realm and called my life quits. Would have solved a lot of problems.

"It is unfortunate your upbringing led you to the path you took in life, but you have a chance to undo all the wrong, to save lives, and appease two nations who have been warring for centuries."

I shook my head ready to tell him off but then thought better of it. I wasn't sure if it was blood loss or just the taxation of using my mothers' gift, but the small voice in the back of my head told me to use this. Use this to my advantage to seek medical treatment, learn about my surroundings and once I could, escape this wretched planet.

"I'm listening."

The old man nodded and struggled to stand up. I rolled my eyes and strode forward grabbing him by the front of his robes, hauling him to his feet. The unsheathing of weapons from their holsters echoed across the expanse of the rapidly darkening rain forest. Releasing the old man gingerly, I took a step back before murmuring. "You looked pathetic."

"And you are a good person."

My bark of laughter startled a flock of rousting birds from the trees above, and they scattered, squawking their complaints to me. I bared my teeth in their direction. I hoped they saw my fangs and knew I was a predator. " I am not a ni—." I swayed falling to a knee and threw my spare hand out, the one not drenched in my own blood, to steady myself.

Shit. Blood loss had finally gotten to me.

The old man's face crumbled in concern, and he motioned to one of the sentinels behind me. "I did not know this was your blood. Why did you not tell me you were injured?"

"It's fine. I've had worse." My words slurred as I tried to shrug off the sentinel's hands on my back. My strength faltered and that was all they needed to gain the advantage.

I let out a hiss, showing them I could still bite if I had to as I was hefted up, arm wrapped around my waist. Another sentinel approached and reached down, grabbing me by my boots.

Right, this was a comfortable way to carry a bleeding person.

"You guys suck at this."

Blood began to run rapidly down my side, a steady stream leaving a trail behind us as we moved forward.

Huh. Maybe this was a little worse than I let on.

I opened my mouth to say something. Something along the lines of maybe they should hold pressure on my wound, but darkness intruded. The last thing I heard before my eyes shut, was the frantic cry from the old man. "Don't let the heir bleed out. We need her to forge the alliance."

I tried to make my lips move, to ask what he meant by heir, but they had gone numb. My eyes refused to open, and I tried to struggle against the tide of unconsciousness pulling me under.

And for the first time in my life I lost, as the darkness fully engulfed me.

Monster in Training

The room grows hazy, smoke rising from my mouth.
A disco light bought at the bazar, authentic from earth they said, flung colors throughout the darkened room.
A thud came from the door, two thuds, now three—sigh.
Slowly, I collect my legs under my body, shaking out my tail behind me.
The door creaks open— my little sister, red in the face, staring at me with her three eyes.
I throw her the finger and slam the door, locking it behind me.
She pounds on the door with her hoof, but I turn up my music and take another hit from the pipe.
I wonder how other life forms deal with family sometimes.
Forever Annoyed,
Monster in Training (I Guess)

Neighborhood Vampire

A pologizes but I do relapse sometimes.
Society has screwed with my headspace for so long that old habits become much harder to break.
Truly, I try but mostly I slide—
right back into the black pit that is my mind.
Truly Yours,
The Friendly Neighborhood Vampire.

Sacrifice

"You see that star coupling to the right? The one that looks like a willow tree. It's commonly known as the Healer's Star."

Aiden's face scrunched up in thought, "Why name it the Healer's star?"

I smiled, as this was one of my favorite tales to tell all the young rovers in my camp.

"Once long ago, an ordinary man had to make a choice. The choice between his life and his heart. You see this man had heard of a tale, one spun long ago. It said when the brightest moon of the year was at its peak, and if you were patient enough to wait, the maiden of the moon would appear, granting you a wish. The only caveat was she would appear on the rocks in the middle of Hunters lake, which had a tale of its own."

I paused making sure Aiden was listening to this next part. " It was called Hunters Lake because of the monster who lived within its depths. Many a proclaimed hero died horrific deaths trying to slay this monster, including a few dragon folk."

Aiden looked at me in surprise before squinting back up to the star, waiting for me to continue.

"Any normal man, human or otherwise would have just laughed off the tale of the moon maiden and went along his merry way. Except for this one. For you see, this one needed a miracle. The man was a father and his child had succumbed to a rare blood illness. He had scoured the entire realm looking for a cure, but there was none to be had. He knew this tale was just that—a tale, but he had nothing to lose the night he rowed the small boat out into Hunters Lake. He waited patiently as the moon reached its peak and waited longer still until dawn was but an hour away.

What he did not know was a monster indeed lurked below; watching—waiting, ready to devour him at any moment. Right when the monster was about to attack, the sounds of soft weeping reached its ears. It became curious as to why this man was not hunting it, as that was what all creatures did when coming to this lake. So instead of attacking, it glided to the surface and perched upon the rocks, waiting for the weeping man to notice it. Notice it the man did, but he did not seem frighten because instead he asked if the monster could help him. The monster took pity upon him, telling the man to come back the next day with his daughter. Little did they know it was already too late, as his daughter had taken her last breath that very night."

Aiden threw a stone into the fire and I stopped talking. "Would you like me to stop?"

Aiden hunched over, angrily poking at the fire with a stick. "No, I want to know what happened to the man and monster."

I smiled and continued.

"Heartbroken, the man came back the next day with his dead daughter. The monster you see was not always a monster. She used to be a great healer of her people before she was cursed to spend eternity rotting away at the bottom of the lake. Over time she grew to despise mankind as they tried to hunt her down, but this man was different. The monster had to be sure though. It told him, to bring his daughters' life back another her age must die. The man, heartbroken and full of grief thanked the monster but politely declined. For he could not put another family through the grief he was feeling. The monster smiled knowing it had chosen wisely.

"*Human,*" the monster called out, "*you are indeed worthy of my gift.*"

The man was confused until the monster lifted its claws, placing them upon his child. With a gasp she awoke, clutching to her father in confusion. The father cried out in happiness as the monster began to change, floating back up to the moon."

"For you see, the monster and the moon maiden were always one in the same, legend becoming distorted over time. And when the man unselfishly made the choice to let his daughter go forever instead of ruining another family, the monster knew this was the man who could break her curse."

"But how?" Aiden interrupted me, then immediately mouthed an apology.

I chuckled. "Sacrifice is a powerful thing. Unselfish acts for the sake of another's happiness is one of the most powerful magics in all the realms."

Aiden squinted into the fire then looked up at me. "What happened to the girl?"

I chuckled as Aiden's mom called out to him. It was far past his bedtime and Aiden sighed before scampering away.

I glanced up to the stars once more and murmured low under my breath. "She became a rover."

ShadowRealm

The wind whipped through my short red hair as I stood on the broken-down high rise. I looked out across the city speckled with broken down buildings and flickering with neon lights. The wind howled around me as I reached up, my hand catching the bit of paper flying past.

45th Burn street.

Like usual no indication on when the soul would depart. I let the paper go, the wind stealing it away to parts unknown. No matter how many times I came up here, I never saw papers littered on the top of the building or on the ground around it. I still didn't know who sent the locations to me. We never got that far in training.

The wind thrashed at my jacket and I grabbed its collar, rubbing my face against the worn leather. It was of course too big for me, zipper broken long ago. I sighed and shoved my hands into the pockets. It was made of real leather, not the fake stuff they started making a few centuries ago. No, this jacket was authentic—a motorcycle jacket, circa 1950's from when he lived as a mortal. I crouched down taking a huge breath of icy air, ignoring the flicker out of the corner of my eye. I buried my face into the collar of the jacket once more, breathing in leather, pine, and wood smoke. I could never figure out why the jacket still smelled of the forest he first died in, but it did.

Sometimes death just remained upon certain items forever, three hundred and fifty-four years in this case.

The clouds passed over the sun slowly, making the shadows on the roof top move. I swore I heard the shuffle of his feet and his disapproving sigh. He never did approve of the clothes I wore while working.

"This isn't a fashion show," he would always complain. *"You need practical clothing to protect you in a fight."*

I would just scoff and say, *"my t shirt and black pants are fine".*

I still wore the t shirt and tight black pants, though now I paired them with leather thigh high boots, and his leather jacket.

Chuckling to myself, I launched my body off the high rise.

He always hated it when I did this. Not because I couldn't die— hard to kill the already dead though not impossible. But because I always insisted on landing in what I called the *superhero* pose. Way to dramatic and attention seeking for my mentor.

This time I landed, rolling with my momentum, and started walking towards Burn Street. I shook my head trying to forget my twice dead mentor. He wasn't coming back this time. Like I said before, it's nearly impossible to kill the already dead, but it can be done, and I was to blame.

I was the one who killed him with my stupidity and arrogant ways.

And now— now, I was walking right back into the fray he lost his life saving me from.

Survival

S he rushes through the tall grass, soft dirt rustling under her paws. Glancing up to the midnight sky, she senses the storm coming.

Faster, faster, she tells herself.

She can smell the intruders. They're close. Their campfire is so close, she can smell the smoke and smolder of pinecones. A low rumble fills her chest as she slinks through the grass and circles the campsite. She can hear them laughing, talking, drinking.

They think they have escaped her. How foolish these amateur hunters are.

She had finally established a normal life, and then, they showed up. Following her, staking out her home, thinking she wouldn't notice them. She has lived this façade for ten human years now, and she refused to start all over again. Her anger mounts and she crawls forward on her belly, getting within killing distance.

Wait — one has left the group.

Good, she thinks, *easy prey.*

Backing up, she sees him pissing next to a tree. One leap, she goes for the throat, he doesn't even scream. Now, for the other two. She is right behind the fools now.

She flies. Claws rip through a chest. Blood splatters against the swaying grass. Her mouth clamps onto a throat, and she shakes until all life has left him. She drops the body and dodges to the right. The other has a knife coated in poison; she can smell it.

Be careful. Think human.

She barrels right into his legs. He goes down hard, knife lost to the tall grass. Stepping on his chest, she bares down and sees the fear reflecting from his eyes. He makes mumbling noises, pleading, begging; yet she must.

She must survive, and to do so, these men had to die.

Saliva drips as she lowers her massive head, and with one swoop she tears out his throat. Blood pours, coating her chest and paws. Turning, she flees, not toward home but to the water she hears. The human within tells her to clean herself, get rid of the evidence.

Evidence? What is that?

The human tries to explain, but she stops listening. The storm finally lets loose, rain seeping into her thick fur. It is time to head home.

She reaches the burrow where the human hid her clothes, a short distance from the lights, loud noises, and foul smelling dwellings. She turns, twisting and changing. Hesitantly, she stands on two legs. Balance was always tricky seconds after the change. She makes haste putting on her t shirt, and sweats. Flipflops in hand, she jogs back to her apartment, fully human now. Barely making a sound, she reaches the shabby apartment building and climbs the fire escape to the window left unlocked. She had to get some sleep because tomorrow was an exciting day.

Tomorrow she starts her new job, with the agency assigned to hunt predators— just like her.

The Dance

Spinning
Faster and Faster.
Faster and Faster.
Stop.
Flash a bit of thigh and toss the hair.
Spin about the other way.
Remember — clap your hands to the beat.
Hips now.
Put your hips into it more.
And try to remember,
you are dancing for your life,
in this post apocalyptic world
we now call a home.

The Drifter

It has taken decades to figure out why I cannot stay in one place for
too long.
At first, I thought it was because my heart longed for a place I had yet
to see.
A place I would instantaneously know once I stumbled upon it.
Which is still possible.
But mostly— I figure the things I seek are the moments in between.
Those little moments you feel when the world takes a collective breath
before everything becomes normal again.
Those little moments, when time comes to a standstill between one
heartbeat and the next,
a picture capturing a memory which only lasts until you take your next
breath.
Those are the moments I will always chase.
And this is why,
I can never stay.

The End

The soft sound of waves lapping against rocks woke me with a jolt, and I sat up quickly.

Mistake.

My head swam, and I clutched at it. The spinning stopped moments later, and I took my hands away from my face.

I frowned, turning them over.

They were wrapped in soft strips of linin, weaving their way up my forearms.

This wasn't right.

Looking down, I noted the white linin dress I was wearing instead of my battle hardened leather. The dress was Grecian in style, long and flowing. I had seen this particular dress before—long, long ago. I just couldn't remember where. Shaking my head, my hair flowed loose in soft waves, the shade natural middle of the road brown, hitting me at my waist.

I reached up touching the right side, fingers sliding against a row of braids. Either I had been in a coma for years, or I was—I shivered and turned, letting my feet dangle off the side of the smooth platform I had awoken on. It was cool to the touch, but I expected nothing else. It was a rock after all.

With a deep breath, I glanced towards the sound of water lapping against the rocks and my breath caught. I was far back in the mouth of a large cavern, butted up against a body of water stretching out as far as I could see. Slowly lowering myself to the ground, my bare feet sunk into the cool onyx sand covering the cavern floor and I padded towards the opening. The sun—no, two suns, dipped below the horizon and the sky lit up in a kaleidoscope of pinks, blues, greens, and purples. Stars began to wink into existence as the suns disappeared entirely, and a broken moon took their place. I took in the sky and the strange world before me, dolphins leaping from watery depths, emerald green flowers blooming around the cave entrance, and crystal white vines wrapped around cherry red tree trunks.

Out of the corner of my eye, a man shimmered into existence like a mirage on the high desert. He was a few inches taller than me, of average build, with long wavy dark blonde hair falling to his shoulders. He stood there silently, hands behind his back, looking out to the dolphins dancing within their watery domain. I waited, oddly calm.

"I always wondered if I would see this place again." The man murmured before turning to me. I couldn't place my finger on it, but deep down I knew this world and man oddly familiar.

He smiled softly at my confusion. "I do believe the words out of your mouth the first time were— *what the fuck am I wearing* ?"

I flinched.

Yes, that sounded like me, but those words coming out of this man just seemed wrong. I stared and he met my eyes without a flinch, a rarity in my life. It looked like I would have to continue the conversation if I wanted answers.

Though, I already had a feeling I knew what had happened.

I looked down at my hands, flexing them. "It's done, isn't it? We lost?"

The man blinked and cocked his head, his form shimmering slightly before solidifying again. "Maybe, but yes— the battle for your world was lost. The reason why you returned the first time is over."

I gaped at him as horror tried to take over my mind. Shaking my head, I looked away just as a dolphin arced through the air as if it were trying to touch the broken pieces of the moon. This couldn't be happening.

"We weren't supposed to lose." I choked on the words, tears threatening to spill down my cheeks.

The man took my hand gently, rubbing my knuckles. "Reyja, I told you before it would be a long painful road to the end. Do you remember what I told you the first time?"

Words echoed through my mind; memory pulled from depths unknown. The words shaped themselves upon my tongue. "Humans, the most stubborn creatures in the universe. They just don't know when to stay down."

He let go of my hand far too quickly and tapped my forehead with his index finger. "Fight."

The world around me exploded in white light and I hit the ground hard, flexing my fingers against dirt, worn leather gloves encasing my hands once more. Strong arms wrapped around my waist, effortlessly crushing me against a hard chest.

A smell I lost three hundred and seventy-five years ago, assaulted my senses.

Leather, pine, and hickory smoke.

Inhaling deeply, tears held back for far too long streaked down my face. "Adam?"

My legs gave out, causing us both to collapse to the ground still holding onto each other. I choked on my words, tears streaming down my face and soaking into Adam's shirt. "I am so sorry. I didn't mean it."

I looked up finally, into a face I dreamed about kissing just one more time. The face I thought about every time I shut my eyes.

"I know you didn't Reyja. If you would have done anything other, it wouldn't have been you."

I shuddered and buried my head into his chest again. I don't know how long we stayed there, clutched to each other but eventually the tears ended, and I shifted slightly taking in my surroundings. I pushed my short, tangled hair out of my eyes, and Adam kissed my temple.

"Hey." It was shaky and cracked but it was still a word.

Adam smiled. "Hey."

"So, what now? Where is here?"

Adam shifted, getting to his feet, and lifting me up easily along with him. I reached up tracing the scar cutting across his face with my fingertips. He caught my hand, interlacing his fingers with mine and took a deep breath. "Nothing Reyja, it's over. There's no going back from here, no more souls to save in that world. No more fight to fight."

I frowned, dropping my hand from his. An echo of a word on the tip of my tongue.

Adam tilted his head studying my face. "That is your '*this is not happening on my watch*' face. What's going on in your head, Reyja?"

I turned, looking behind me into a darkened forest before facing back towards Adam. "What if it isn't over though? What if—." I looked down flexing my hand open then close.

"Reyja?"

I glanced up and Adam stepped forward, gently grabbing my upper arm. I shook my head and stepped closer, resting my head on his chest. "I just have this echo in my head is all."

Adam stroked my hair, "We all do Reyja. The afterlife is not as restful as one would think."

I shook my head looking into the darkness of the wood again. Slipping my hand into Adam's, he tugged me forward with him down a well-worn dirt path.

The word, *fight* faded out of existence from the back of my mind.

The General

I watch her from my porch. Same time every week, three times a week she walks by.

Brown hair swinging just the same with every step, sun glinting off freckled cheeks. I lift my beer in salute and nod my head to her.

She smiles, never showing her teeth and nods in return, continuing her path.

I watch, scanning the street. My ears perk up in the direction of some punks standing near the liquor store, cat calling her as she passes by. She ducks her head and carries on with her mission.

Always the same grocery store, three times a week. Same time, every day.

I take note of the cat callers, memorizing their faces. They are young, unknowing in their treason. They will learn not to bother her again.

I wait.

An hour passes.

There she is, like clockwork, walking back up the street. Her reusable bag is full this time, our usual greeting commences again. And again, like the days and weeks before, I watch her walk to the rundown apartment building. She goes inside, door creaking shut behind her.

TWO MONTHS HAVE PASSED since she and a male entity moved into the apartment. I see him from my porch every afternoon when he comes out to smoke and talk to the punks hanging out front.

I don't care for him.

SOMETHING IS NOT RIGHT.

A week has passed by and I have not seen her.

I know I did not miss her. My men inform me she is still around but hasn't left the building.

Another week passes by.

There she is, but she is walking on the other side of the street. Head tucked, she does not look up. She does not acknowledge me.

I get off my porch this time, crossing the street to wait. An hour passes and there she is, walking towards me. She gets closer and stops—inches away. No sound arises from either of us as I put my finger under her chin and lift her face. I turn away, crossing the street and walk back to my porch. I sit and watch her walk to her building, back to the man who gave her the fading bruises across her sun kissed face.

I WATCH HER FROM MY porch.

Same time every week; walking to the grocery store. Except this time, she starts and ends at my porch. She smiles fully and the golden spark lying behind her eyes is prominent now. The man is gone. She comes to me, asking how long I knew.

I tell her.

"From the moment they moved into the building."

She looks me dead in the eyes and asks about herself.

I shrug and ask a question in kind, "Do you enjoy it? Being bait?"

She dips her head as to shy away from the question but finds her resolve. "Not even for a second," She murmurs.

vered claws, scratching at the onyx surface we were standing on. It was the only color, as the hound in front of me was blacker than an abyss itself. An abyss being the only thing I could think to compare it to. I couldn't quite figure out if it was more canine or feline, so my mind settled on both. Sucking in a tepid breath, the hound stalked closer.

The drawings in the old books didn't hold a candle to the hound in front of me. The hound within me, the hound who gave me—no, made me everything I was.

I shook my head, no— that was not right. It gave me some things, but not all. I held onto that thought.

The hound smiled, teeth razor sharp and the size of my fingers. Its coat shimmered but I couldn't quite place if it was black skin or coated in some sort of silken, inky black fur.

"Hellhound." My voice was steady even though I was shaking inside.

Hellhounds, from what I had read were strong, fast, and deadly. They were guardians of the Banished Realm and here one was, taking up residence in my mind. Steam twisted out of the hellhounds mouth as it laughed with the most beautiful voice I had ever heard before. Feminine in nature, but I learned early on applying gender to a creature from another realm was hit or miss. The hellhound sat, steam rolling off from— now that it was closer, a coat of fur akin to that of a big cat. Heat licked out and I had to control myself from stepping away. Oh, and let's not acknowledge the fear radiating through my whole body screaming for me to run. I mentally slapped myself and the hellhound smiled, as if it knew.

"If that is what you would like to label me as, you may."

I blinked.

Wait, was it saying it wasn't? I guess I could ask.

"Then what type of creature are you?"

At least my mouth was still working, curiosity winning out over fear. The hellhounds tail swished lazily back and forth, catching my attention. It was soothing in a weird way.

"We are many different kinds, but the same species if you may call us that."

I didn't dare make a sound, waiting for it to continue.

"We live in what you call the Banished Realm. If you choose to call our realm, Hell, like the generations before you did then yes, I would be a hellhound."

I racked my brain trying to remember what I could about the Banished realm, and Hell. I knew it housed the dead but also, "Demons?"

It stared at me intently and the question I really didn't want the answer to came out. "... and you inhabit my body. For how long?"

The hound smiled and slowly circled me, claws scraping against the smooth floor. It chuckled.

"How long?" The whisper of hot breath scalded the back of my neck. "Since the day you were born, young one. We are two souls as one, and we will stay this way until our last breath."

I turned, facing its muzzle, nose to nose. I ground my teeth. " So am I a demon then? Of the Banished Realm?"

The hound chuckled, the smell of ozone filling the air. "Yes, maybe." It frowned. "We originated from there yes, but you were born here. In the realm you live in now." The hound took a step back and sat, "Your family, my family was slaughtered. In the times before and now, the human hunters always feared those to be more powerful than they."

I flinched, but kept my eyes locked with the hounds. It turned away looking up at the stars. "We used to look at the stars like this, you and I, together in the camp. Before they came, killing all around them. Yes, we were more powerful but that—" It growled suddenly, eyes flashing bright, and I took a hasty step back. "That is the downfall, is it not. Lest we forget arrogance is what kills. Humans are smart and made weapons to take away our power, putting us to sleep and keeping only the human half awake."

It shook its head, as if shaking the memory from its mind. " We were young, that is what saved us. Not even a year old. Taken from a dead woman's grasp."

I swallowed and the hound glanced at me. "Why—why now? Why didn't you make yourself known sooner?"

It laughed, and tilted its head, "Katrina."

I took a step back at the mention of my sister's name, " What of my sister?" I demanded, hand flexing in anger. My temper flared and the hound rose, facing off with me.

"I made a deal with your sister, but she is gone, and I can no longer keep true to our deal. Nor can I keep to the pact you demanded of me the night after she left."

The anger building in my chest billowed out of existence, and my knees gave out on me. "I knew there was something—I just , I just..." My voice cracked as a single tear fell, dropping on my outstretched hand.

The hound stalked forward. " I know. I deceived you. We all did. When your sister found out what you were, she—" The hound stopped mid-sentence and I looked up at it.

"What did she do?" I ground out.

The hound looked at me and I swear I saw pain in its eyes. "Your sister cared. She never saw us as a monster, or a pet. She just cared for us—as a true family would."

I opened my mouth about to demand more. I still couldn't understand how I had been kept in the dark of my true nature for so long, but fate decided it was time to intervene.

The hound snapped its teeth, looking behind me. " Wake up. Wake up now."

I blinked—wait, what?

It snarled at me, "Something has changed. You— we are not safe."

I locked eyes with the hound once more, and it strode forward. "We will continue our conversation later."

I nod.

Yes, we definitely needed to speak again later. I took a deep breath centering myself to wake.

" Wait..."

I opened my eyes, the hound's snout inches away from my nose.

" Just—whatever happens, know we are one. Use and trust in my—our abilities. Make your way back here when it is safe."

The hound glanced up at the stars, "There is so much more you—we still need to know."

I reached out instinctually as the hound started to dissipate, and everything turned to dust around me.

The Moon

Once long ago, two members of opposing fae factions fell in love.
And as we know these stories never have happy endings.
As one might guess, their love was discovered and the lovers were
pulled apart,
to be placed under a curse.
The woman, with skin as translucent as the moon, and billowing silver
hair was transformed into her name sake,
the moon itself,
to forever stare down upon her lover.
Her lover transformed into a beast,
to forever run on all fours,
and to be driven mad by his love for the moon.
And for years this was so, but as time passed,
strange powers amassed and the moon became an idol.
Worshipped in her beauty and splendor.
Soon her powers grew.
Then one fateful eve, when peril was about to overcome her one true
love,
she willed herself into fae form once more
stepping down from the stars to save him.
And when their hands touched for the first time in centuries,
madness left his soul and he transformed into a man once more.
But her powers were drained,
and she could only hold her form for a single night.
So, she vowed.
Once every month at her peak,

when she was full and bright in the sky,
she would return to earth to be with him,
her true love
if only for one night.
But before she left,
she imparted him with a gift.
Though not powerful enough to lift the curse from them, she could
lessen it, oh so slightly.
She lifted his madness, granting him the power to change at will.
He was still a beast,
but could choose to be man if he so pleased.
And so, the legend of the werewolf was born.
And if you find yourself deep within the wood, and the moon is shining bright,
close your eyes and listen.
Listen, as we worship our mother in our own right.
For she was the first,
forever protecting and blessing us,
her children of the night.

The Old Brick Road

You told me to follow the old brick road and I would find my way
home.
What you did not tell me though, was who I would meet along the
way
and how it would change me down to the very fabric of my soul.
You did not tell me of the beast who lived deep in the wood,
the one everyone feared but deep down,
he only needed someone to care.
Nor did you tell me of the man— the man who stole hearts
because he never knew the concept of love.
But you did warn me of the witch who lived in her tower,
all alone and despised by all.
You told me,
avoid the witch at all costs for her power is too great.
I did not heed your warning.
For I found out a witch she was only in name,
given by the men she left scorned and broken
when they tried to steal her power away.
And when I happened upon her
waiting for me at the end of the old road,
I did not run.
For, I did not fear her.
Instead, I glimpsed a part of myself reflecting within her soul.
She welcomed me with open arms and
gladly sent me home,
without mere riddle or dangerous quest.

And the pretty boy behind me, you ask?
The one with straw colored hair and eyes as blue as the sky on a cloud-
less summer day.
He only wanted someone to look past his beautiful shell to see the
magnificent and complex mind shining out.
So yes, the story was wrong.
I was never interested in a pretty pair of shoes.
The lion was never a coward, but a beast of a man who cared far too
much.
The tin man stole women's hearts and buried them in the apple or-
chard.
The scarecrow was only seen as a pretty face, until he showed you his
intellect burning bright within his eyes.
And, as far as the evil witch goes—
You should never judge a book by its cover.
It was the good witch who gave me riddles,
and sent me down the brick road to certain doom.
And it was your evil witch who welcomed me into her tower with
open arms,
and gave me what I wanted all along—
A way home.

The Order

In the aftermath of the unveiling,
destruction and chaos rang throughout major cities in the America's and
Central Europe.
Humans now survive in groups on the outer limits of major cities,
because to stray too close to the others meant certain death, or for the un-
lucky few,
un-death.

A warm summer wind whipped around David as he hunkered down, pulling his leather jacket tighter around his body. Four hours had passed since he had been given his orders. Orders to find and extract the soul; unfortunately, they never came with a time.

David frowned at the paper in his hand with the name of the club scribbled on it. That was it— the location, not even a clue to what his assignment looked like.

"A gender or even a description of what they are wearing would have been helpful." He grumbled, shoving the paper back into his pocket.

David squinted, watching as two humans and one of the undead entered the club. "Reckless," he scoffed into the wind before standing up to stretch his legs.

He had no worry about the bloodsuckers seeing him; he had picked his location carefully on the high rise across from the club. The undead bloodsuckers had become used to being the biggest predator around, so much so, security was lacking. Even if they did spot him, they wouldn't care. Only a select few people in the world had the knowledge, strength, and ability to kill them. Even David didn't have the ability to kill the bloodsuckers. Sure, he could easily incapacitate them, but to truly kill one— you had to have the ability to wield soul fire. And that wasn't a skill someone could just learn. For soul fire to be used effectively, it had to be a gift from *Death* itself.

The clicking of a woman's heels on the uneven sidewalk below shook David out of his brooding. Looking to his left, he glimpsed a vision of beauty, encased in a dark red silk dress, approaching the side door of the club. As the door creaked opened letting her in, she turned—and looked right at him with the most vivid green eyes he had ever beheld in his one hundred and fifty years.

She turned away and stepped over the threshold.

David let out the breath he didn't even know he was holding, and his gut twisted knowing deep down, she was his assignment. David found himself wishing, for the first time in his life, that he didn't have to wait until her death to save her.

LEANING OVER THE WOMAN'S body six hours later in the alley behind the club, David glanced into once vivid green eyes— now milky in death. He scowled at the thoughts of what they had done to her. Cradling her gently against his body, David scaled the stairs of the next door apartment building, abandoned to everyone except the few wild dogs making their inhabitance downstairs.

Reaching the rooftop, he sat, laying her cooling body beside him and her hair cascaded around her body like a golden waterfall. He weaved his fingers through it, feeling the disfigured bones in her neck. The undead had snapped it when they had finished with her.

Growling in frustration, David shook his head to clear his mind and let out a soft sigh of relief as the first rays of morning light peeked over into the alley. He would be safe pulling her soul back for now. The bloodsuckers would be dormant because of the early hour, and the wild animals living below would too, be resting.

Closing his eyes, David hovered his hand over the woman's chest and plunged his mind into the afterlife, crossing his spirit over to find the gatekeeper.

The first time he had crossed over was with his own death, and what he discovered over the years, was the afterlife changed constantly. The first time, D*eath* had molded itself around his beliefs and showed him what he had wanted to see. Later, after his rebirth, he discovered what he experienced was only the first plane of death. The best thing about this plane—time was suspended here. When he was dead for approximately thirty minutes in his world, he was on this side for over a year—training for his duties before he could leave.

Opening his eyes after what felt like an eternity, David found himself standing on a riverbank, his back against a forest of silver trees. He turned slowly at the sound of rustling leaves, and a beautiful silken voice rang out.

"What took you so long?" The woman in the red dress called to him with a smirk, closing the book in her hand with an audible snap.

David lifted an eyebrow. "How long?" He asked, knowing she had only been dead for a total of fifteen minutes.

"Two and a half years," she sighed, before looking up at the light pink sky. "I'm Cassie by the way."

"Well, Cassie," David murmured and reached his hand out to the woman in red. "Let's get you back to the real world and see what you can do for Death's Order."

Clasping his hand in hers, Cassie flashed David with a wolfish grin and picked up the sword by her side. A silvered mist trickled across the grounds and fully engulfed their bodies, shifting them back into the world of the living.

The Patient

Mental illness is an utterly unique type of monster.
Afflicting all and sinking its fingers into anything it can without dis-
crimination.
It's not the type of thing you can face head on.
No, mental illness is a parasite riding your mind like a beast of burden,
slowly crumbling your stone walled defenses.
It's the type of evil whispering cloying animosities in the back of your
mind,
breaking down your self esteem one notch at a time.
And every time you fight it and win,
it just comes back like a drug resistant strain.
And in the end,
you need to believe you are stronger than it,
the next time it comes around.
For it doesn't matter what galaxy or realm you call home,
mental illness will always find a way to damage you.

The Predator

"How do you like being hunted for once?" I whisper slyly to the man in front of me, stalking forward over the slick water-stained rocks. The man groans and scrambles back, blood oozing down his pallor face.

A smile morphs across mine, stopping him in his tracks, "—the prey. Did you ever think you would be such?"

The man shakes his head.

"Do not be afraid to be the prey. It is a good thing," I growl and the man stares at me blankly. I really did a number on him and he wasn't going to last long.

That was okay. I just wanted him to hear this next part before I took his life from him, like how he had tried to take mine.

"How so you might ask?" I purr and crouch, blood caressing my fingers as I reach out smoothing back his hair. I bring them to my lips, tongue darting out to taste copper and I scent the fear wafting from his body. "Let me share a secret with you. As a predator, you see the prey and you want it. You assume we—the predators, take whatever we want but you are wrong. There are two types of predators, the well satisfied and the starved. You assume again the well satisfied predator is the strong one, the better one. Wrong once more. It is the starved one to be wary of. They are the ones who always push the limits. The well satisfied predator will never push limits. They will never take the chance to try for something bigger and stronger. They will stay with the familiar. The starving predator on the other hand, they will never know satisfaction. They will forever push the limits, hunting for the perfect prey.

You see, the prey is the one in power, continually teasing the predator. We can not live without you. You should feel happy, you are wanted, needed. Without you, I would die. Only you, the prey can quench the predator's thirst— their desire, and thrill of the chase. And sometimes..." I reach out grasping the man's throat, "the chase is just thrilling enough to give the starving predator a glimpse of satisfaction."

A gurgle fills the silence of the night and I stand over the lifeless form of the man's body. I waited for the satisfaction to come but like always— I felt nothing.

The Rogue Reaper

And what was the question every sentient creature asked?
Across the universe on every planet?
Millions of languages, shaping words to fall from their lips.
It was always the same question.
What was it again?
Oh yes, how could I forget.
It was always—
Why me?
Never Faltering,
The Rogue Reaper

The Seer

*S*ilently crawling through the rain soaked land, mud splatters onto my face and sweat drips down my back. My muscles were working overtime. I took a deep breath, launching on top of my prey. He never stood a chance. None of them ever did. The brush moved to my right and I dropped silently to the ground, bloodied knife in hand. I was exhausted, running on fumes. I should have run with the rest of them—even our trained killers ran but no, I had to be stubborn about this. Sucking in a deep breath, the stink of swamp water and decaying flesh reached my nose. One of the scouts was close.

Good. That meant I could send a message.

My feet never made a sound, and I was behind the scout, locking it into a choke hold. "Listen carefully," I whisper, face so close to its rotting flesh, I almost vomited. It stilled, knowing not to fight back. Scouts were weak, I found this out long ago. Even a changed human like myself could overpower one easily. I tighten my arm and it let out a squeak, "Are you listening?"

"Yessss," It hissed.

I suppressed my shiver at the sound of its voice. If snakes could talk, I always imagined this was what they sounded like.

"Good, tell your master I am coming for him, and make sure he is prepared for the bloodbath I will leave in my wake." I push the scout away, the want to bury my dagger deep into its back an insatiable ache but I held back. It loped away, getting smaller and smaller until finally disappearing into the approaching mist. I let out a growl, closing my eyes as the fine mist wrapped itself around my form, pulling me back into reality.

THE WARM AND STEADY hands on my shoulders felt like heaven, and I sucked in a deep breath before opening my eyes. I couldn't help my smile as I gazed at the strong handsome face in front of me. Dansic's dark brown eyes were full of warmth and worry.

"There you are Lauren." He murmured, before leaning back in his chair, pushing back his newly dyed, and shockingly bright, purple hair.

I would never tell him how much it suited his personality. I should have before— I shook my head, lingering remains of my vision in the forefront of my mind. Frowning, I wondered where that thought had come from and in the pit of my stomach, I knew something was about to happen. "Dansic..." I managed to choke out his name before the overwhelming stink of swamp water and decaying flesh assaulted my senses. Sound seemed to sway, silence engulfing the massive room as the tavern door exploded open. Shock framed my face and Dansic's expression hardened before he flew across the table, taking me down to the floor. Time warped and screaming— the sound of fighting, assaulted my senses all at once.

And this time, I knew my vision was about to come true.

The Siren

Water cresting.
Riding the wave.
Diving below at just the right moment,
before the current pulls you under.
Again, and again ... until I can get it just right.
Day and night the waves change under the moon,
sometimes calm and at other times, crashing like thunder upon the
cliff face.
I will ride the wave again tomorrow.
I'm sure of it.
Because what else is there to do with this endless life I live?
Forever Yours,
The Siren.

The Tavern

Andie kicked her feet up onto the sticky bar table. The barkeep and owner of the tavern, Wiggins, stood in front of the bar top instead of behind, surveying the mess. Broken chairs, tables, and glass littered the entire tavern and the chandelier above was hanging precariously by its chain.

"Andie, get up off your ass and help." The call came from a gruff looking man, over six feet tall with shaggy, unkept hair. He was employed here as a bouncer, the good it did for them. Normally the town only ever had minor bar disagreements, except for when *they* showed up.

"Ian, you know this ass doesn't clean." Andie growled settling into her chair, yanking her warm beanie down over her short black curly hair to obscure her view of the room.

"Andie—."

It was Wiggins's sigh that had Andie sighing herself, before getting up. She stalked over to the side of the bar and grabbed the broom. "Fine—see, I'm helping. But take note I am very much against manual labor."

"Thank you." Wiggins murmured, before walking away to help Ian try to put the door back on its hinges.

"What in all the Realms happened this time around?" Andie called out over her shoulder.

"It was just a bunch of locals until the fucking guild and their stupid party showed up." Ian grunted out as he held the door in place.

"No," Andie exclaimed, whipping around to face them. "Wiggins you said the *Party of the Dead Badger* was no longer allowed to set foot in our establishment. Not after last time."

"Andie, you know business has been trying."

Andie motioned around the tavern with her broom, "Bodies Wiggins. There were bodies swinging from the antler chandelier last time. How could you think letting them back in would be good for the tavern?"

Wiggins's shrugged and continued to nail the door back up. Andie rolled her eyes and got back to sweeping but not before she mumbled under her breath, "At least they didn't burn this one to the ground."

Ian let out a bark of laughter before stepping away from the door. This time it was Andie's turn to laugh as she turned around. The door was hanging skewed. "Nice door Wiggins. Should keep out all the rift raff."

"Hush you. Your sass is noted." Wiggins grumbled under his breath before stalking back over to the bar. Normally anyone in his predicament would pour himself a drink but Wiggins didn't drink.

Funny really. A barkeep who was sober.

The thump of the door falling off its hinges and landing on the ground was to much and Andie began to laugh so hard, tears ran down her face.

"What am I going to do?" Wiggins pleaded and motioned around the tavern. "I don't have funds to repair this entire place. All the glasses and alcohol are smashed, the door is destroyed, and the only thing the tables and chairs are good for anymore is kindling."

Andie took pity on Wiggins and gave him a soft smile. He was after all her father, and this establishment would be hers after he retired. That is, if it didn't get destroyed by guild parties in the meantime.

"Here Pop." Andie extended her hand, and with it a coin pouch.

Wiggins glanced over, then did a double take before stalking over to Andie. "Daughter, you didn't."

Andie shrugged, "I saw them walking into town this morning. I followed the knight and royal into a shop. It wasn't too hard to take it from them."

Wiggins shook his head, pushing Andie's fingers around the pouch. "Tavern be damned. We always rebuild. The town can help us out. No, we will use this money to get your brother out of jail."

Andie smiled and put the coin purse back into her coat pocket. Picking up the broom once more, she glanced over her shoulder again as Ian tried putting the door right side up and her father strolled through the mess of tables and chairs to see what could be salvaged.

Damn, Andie thought with a smile, *it was good to be home.*

The Tired Traveler

The sound of caravan wagons packing up for the night echoed across
the expanse of the desert.
I take in the smells and the sounds as we walk by.
A trader waves as we walk to the portal, and his family asks if we need
anything for our journey.
I smile and reply, not today but maybe next time.
Their murmured thanks turn into background noise as we step into
line.
I glance back in longing, watching as they move across the desert to an
oasis far off in the distance.
A small tent city under the endless night sky.
They will be back this way the next day.
As galaxy waystations go, this one is nice.
Caravans peddling and trading goods,
one of the few ways to make a living now a day.
Selling goods to travelers—enforcers like us.
I step through the portal and wonder briefly if they ever grow tired of
being stuck on this one tiny planet.
I frown, stepping back into the bustling sky city headquarters called
home.
Perhaps I should have stayed,
taking them up on their offer to sit around a campfire watching the
endless stars scattered across the emerald green night sky.
I sigh.
In another lifetime,
perhaps I could have stayed.

The Waystation

You know the waystation—the one in the middle of nowhere within
the Aevarat Galaxy?
The one shimmering like an oasis popping up so unexpectedly in the
middle of the desert.
The one you desperately needed at this exact moment in life.
I know it's illogical but most the time,
I feel like I'm this temporary waystation.
The one you need,
the one you will only stop at temporarily
before you go on your merry way.
And I often wonder if people see me this way too,
or
do they only realize it after they leave?
But I see it as they enter my life,
the need to take a temporary hiatus from the present.
And I often wonder why I allow this, knowing full well they will al-
ways leave.
Then I wonder why.
Will I never leave the waystation on the farthest outskirts of this
galaxy?
The waystation I've fondly called home,
for far too long.

The Wood

They told me — never stray from the path.
For beyond the path wolves wait for young pretty little things like me.
So pretty and innocent, they used to all say.
I listened and grew,
following the well cobbled path in front of me through the woods.
And as I flourished from girl to maiden,
I met many a man I considered wolves along this cobbled path.
Then one day instead,
I chose to step off the path,
for I could not believe something worse could be hiding in the wood.
It was then, I learned of real wolves and beasts.
Those in human and animal form alike.
And it was there,
I discovered I could be the queen of wolves, to
run wild among the beasts of the wood.
So, now I sit on my thrown among the wolves
and beasts of the wild,
waiting for the innocent to realize
the path was always a trap,
and freedom awaits deep within the wood.

Till Death Do Us Part

The ground shifted as Hadrian's breath left my neck. A sickening crack filled the air and my head hit the pavement. I could feel the thudding of music through the ground from the club as my body lay limp on the pavement.

I struggled to speak, but nothing came out except a trickle of blood and a sharp breath. My head rolled, cheek hitting the cold, cracked pavement. Blood pooled into my hair tinting it red.

I smiled slightly; I would have looked surprisingly good as a red head. Hadrian knelt, knee in my blood. He grabbed my hair, lifting my head up. "Oh, my dear Adeline, do you know that you are dying?"

Laughing, he shook me like a rag doll. "I can't hear you breathing, dear one. This is why we can't be together— too fragile." He let go, my head once more hitting the ground with some force, but I couldn't feel it.

I couldn't feel much of anything anymore.

Hadrian jerked around and hissed as a shadow appeared down the alleyway. I struggled to take another breath, but nothing happened. It was okay though.

A cracking sound burst through the night, making my eyelids open. A breeze floated through the air as darkness covered me. I was getting heavy, and my eyes fluttered closed, everything going black. I hadn't been expecting to die by the hand of the one I thought loved me. The last of my breath left me just as a curse echoed from above, and a volley of bullets ripped into Hadrian's chest.

The smile caressed my lips as I used the last of my strength to open my eyes, and watch my traitorous love die alongside me.

Times Three

The forecast called for a heavy downpour tomorrow, but Grace didn't care. What she cared about was the forecast tonight, calling for heavy snow. This was what they were waiting for. Grace and her friends would be traveling the forest paths tonight in the light of the full moon.

Tonight was special as Grace, Willow, and Adele would be turning eighteen at midnight. Everyone assumed they were sisters but really, they only just met this year. A chance encounter from their point of view, as all three of their families moved to the same small village at the same time. After meeting during the beginning of the school year, they decided to spend their eighteenth birthday together— the snow and full moon a present just for them. Little did they know what would happen at the stroke of midnight.

For one was to become lost, one to be changed, and the last, to be exiled into insanity.

Changed

Riley didn't notice the rain. It wasn't like he cared anyway, today was shaping up to be a crappy day either way. Riley and the pack had found one of the creatures, what was commonly referred to as a mermaid but what the pack called, Sirens.

Adele was her name and by the moon goddess above, she was beautiful.

Her hair was a deep mahogany, with dark red undertones. It cascaded over her shoulders, bringing out the tint of light pink across her nude torso and blended into the blood red of her tail. A locket of burnished silver hung around her neck, settling perfectly between her small breasts.

Riley stared at the engraving, worn down, scarcely making out a heart with a dagger plunged within. *What an odd thing to engrave on a locket*, Riley thought silently.

He shook his head looking away. He shouldn't be committing her beauty to memory.

It would just hurt more when she died.

Everyone knew when you took a siren out of the water for even a minute, they could no longer breathe under it. Unfortunately, plucking sirens from the water had become a sport for them, the pack.

Our only excuse—Sirens were stupid creatures who only knew how to breed and drown people, other creatures— even wolves when they got too close to the water's edge. They couldn't be reasoned with. This one though...

Riley met Adele's eyes. Normally, sirens had cold dead black eyes. Adele though, her eyes were forest green, and they brimmed with something Riley couldn't put his finger on. He looked away quickly. It had to be a trick of some kind, but he couldn't help but feel sorry for them or at least this one. He would never voice his opinion though.

Wolves were ruthless, and the strongest among all the creatures in this world. If they showed any type of mercy, the others— vampires, witches, demons... take your pick, would challenge them for rule. Which would lead to a war Riley didn't want to fight in, not again. The pack barely made it out alive last time.

Markus snapped his fingers and Cooper let out a wicked growl, making Riley jump and tear his eyes away from Adele. He looked to Markus, his alpha, purposely ignoring Cooper and the creepy smile plastered across his face.

"It's time," Markus growled.

Riley nodded at the command and put the car in drive, slowly rolling their way down the pier. A short time later he gently stepped on the brakes and glanced into the rearview mirror once more. Adele met his eyes as Cooper roughly grabbed her by the arm and yanked her out of the car. Riley got out last, trailing a few feet behind. He hated this part, but the rest of the pack loved it.

Speaking of the rest of the pack, they were all waiting at the edge of the pier and Riley took his place in the back, amongst the rest of the lower ranking wolves. He was still a pup after all. If you wanted to call seventeen a pup. He barely suppressed his flinch as the splash of water echoed across the darkness.

First, the siren would try to breathe underwater, not understanding why she no longer could. They always came back up confused but would try again... and again...and again until they passed out. The pack would watch, laughing at the creature's confusion. They would smile and joke as they got back into their vehicles, and Riley would laugh and smile with them. Yet inside his heart would be breaking from the inhumanity of it all.

"Someday", he thought, *"Someday the abuse would stop. Someone will step up and end this madness."*

The sound of thrashing water dissipated. Only the echo of laughter remained, as the pack meandered away, and Riley stood alone on the pier. Looking up to the full moon, he swore he heard the echo of the goddess voice, *"It could have been you. You could be the one."*

Riley shook his head and shuffled forward, watching as the lifeless siren sank into depths unknown within the cold inky blackness of the bay. *"Maybe"*, Riley thought, *"maybe next time he could stop the madness."*

Lost

The wind shattered against the trees with the force of a gods wrath, hail plummeting from the sky hitting the ground with force akin to a rockslide. Everyone was at home; sitting next to the warm fire, curled up under deerskin blankets, all but one.

Grace was alone, frightened, and lost. She had been told to wait here for the hunting party. It was an honor her stepmother said, to sit with the other women, waiting for the men to return with the annual kill. Then it would be up to them—the women, to skin, prepare, and carry meat back. The meat, which would provide the tribe food for the coming winter months. Yet here she was alone, lost in the forest.

Grace had known better then to wander off the path, but she wanted to watch. She wanted to see how the men hunted. It was a sin to think those thoughts. Grace's stepmother had warned her.

She was right.

It was a sin, and Grace was being punished. The cracking of tree branches from above had Grace running from under her temporary shelter into the storm. Lightning crackled across the sky illuminating Grace's surroundings briefly, and she stumbled, unsure of her surroundings. Darkness intruded once more, and Grace flinched as hot breath whispered across the back of her neck.

The growl from behind sent a shiver down her spine. "Are you lost, or did you purposely go hunting for the monster living in the woods?"

"Lost," Grace croaked out, squeezing her eyes shut as the monster sank its teeth into the back of her neck. She felt her blood start to swell, seeping out of the bite mark.

"Do you want to stay lost in the woods, little one?" The monster waited for her answer, claws gripping tight to Graces waist, puncturing the soft flesh of her stomach.

She slowly opened her eyes, looking into the inky blackness of the sky above her. Sinful thoughts rose to the forefront of her mind, and Grace thought back to why she really strayed from the path this morning. Was it to watch the men hunt or was it she, who went hunting for something much more sinful?

The monster leaned down, lapping at the blood trickling from Grace's neck. She felt its smile caress her skin before she answered, as if it knew her mind already.

"Yes," She whispered, "Yes, I think I would like to stay lost."

The monster chuckled, and Grace closed her eyes once more, allowing the monster to grip her tight and show Grace exactly what happened to sinners like her, who decide to stay lost within the wood.

Insanity

The dripping of blood and tears splashing down echoed against the backdrop of her mind. Willow spun around and around, frantically looking for someone to help but no one could help her. Not where she was.

So deep—trapped inside her mind where no one could ever reach her. Blood and tears oozed from her soul, pooling up inside of her until she drowned once more, choking to death on her own insanity for all eternity.

To Help a Demon

Candlelight flickered, and a shiver crawled down my spine. I glanced up nervously from the letter I was reading for the tenth time, whilst hiding in the corner of the study room. The shadow in front of me moved again, morphing into the shape of a body. The candle flickered once more, shadows dancing across ruby red eyes. My breath caught, hand fisting around the letter. The crinkling of paper did nothing to break the building tension. I waited with bated breath and wondered if I had made a terrible mistake.

The demon stepped out of the darkness to meet me.

It always looked like my sister. It was my sister, but only part of the time. Even if I hadn't met her eyes, the way it held itself—lounging against the wall, would have clued me in. It was a type of lounge my strait-laced sister could never achieve. My sister was not in charge tonight.

A slow grin slid across her lips and the demon waited for me to get my fear under control. My fist softened around the letter, and I took a tiny shuffle forward. The demon mimicked me, and all the courage I mustered up, plummeted away.

Time to not be a coward Josephine, I thought silently, as my throat grew drier by the second.

Seconds ticked by as the demon waited for me to decide what I wanted to do. It was not my sister I needed to talk to tonight. It was her other half, the demon living inside. After all, I did ask for this clandestine meeting.

I pushed down my rising panic in fear the demon could feel my emotion through our bond. The bond was something only I and my sister's demon knew about, and its strangled hold it had on the two of us. The letter I held in my hand confirmed many of my suspicions including the bond, but I had to be completely sure.

"Is she conscious?" My voice came out low, whispered —and a lot steadier than I thought I could have mustered in the moment.

The demon leaned its back against the wall once more, a type of liquid relaxation you never saw in humans, and I found myself curious. Her smile was unnerving though, too many teeth showing. Her gaze swept up my body and I fought against the urge to fidget and run away. "She is asleep."

I flinched as the demon's voice filtered out of my sister's throat. I had only heard it a handful of times, but it still got to me. Everyone assumed a demon's voice would be harsh, thick, and deep. Evil—like many of the beings from the Banished Realm are. Instead, her voice trickled into the darkness like dripping honey.

It was a type of voice you wanted to wrap around you like a blanket on a cold winter's night in front of a fireplace. It was comforting and dangerous, as it made me want to trust the demon possessing my sister. Time ticked by as we both stood still, staring, waiting for the other to start.

"Thank you, by the way."

I startled as the demon broke the silence. "Thank you for what?" I whispered looking down the halls to make sure no one could overhear our conversation.

She waved her hand halfheartedly in the direction I was looking. "Don't worry. Everyone is asleep. We are alone."

The way she said 'we are alone' had me stiffening against the wall at my back. This wasn't a good idea. What had I been thinking?

Sucking in my breath harshly, the demon locked eyes with me and took a step forward, raising my sister's hand. The heavy pounding of my heart was all I could hear as her fingers flicked over the edge of my ear, swiping back bits of hair, which had haphazardly fallen into my face.

"I know it's hard to believe, but I cannot—will not hurt you. You can trust in this truth completely."

I sucked in another harsh breath and tried to look everywhere but the demon's eyes. "That is why I needed to speak to you."

I held up the strangled letter.

She plucked it from my hand and took a step back, eyes skimming across it quickly. The second the demon's attention lifted from me, my body slumped against the wall in relief. I wanted to slide all the way to the floor but locked my knees instead, as curiosity got the better of me and I watched the demon.

My sisters upper lip twitched as she turned the letter over, reading the back half. Hesitantly, I reached into my mind and caressed the bond flowing between us. My curiosity wanted to see if I could pick up on any lingering emotions. Most of the time it was the other way around—the demon picking up on my emotions. Always able to track down my whereabouts but every so often, I could pick up on her emotions and whereabouts. I had only done so by mistake a handful of times, but from what I could remember it only happened under extreme stress.

Out of the corner of my eye, I saw the demon smirk as I tugged on the bond. There was nothing and I frowned in disappointment.

Quickly changing my face back to neutral nothingness, the demon looked up and handed the letter back to me with a grimace. "He is right you know."

I blinked as her words registered. "Right about what? That you are dangerous? That eventually you, the thing lingering inside my sister like a parasite, will take full control. Or perhaps I should run and find a way to break ties with the family and the bond tying us together."

The words rushed out of my mouth like a dam breaking, heat rising to my cheeks as I let all my confusion and hurt race down our bond. I wanted it to know exactly what I was feeling. If I had not been watching intently, I would have missed the look of shock quickly flash across my sister's face. Then just like that, the relaxed grin appeared once more like nothing had happened.

Her blink was slow, and I held my breath trying to fight my rising anger. "Yes."

All my anger deflated, sadness filtering across my chest. The demon sighed and in the rare few times I had seen it in control, it portrayed a very human trait. The demon rubbed at its eyes and exhaustion racked its next words.

"Yes, I am dangerous, but you and the family already know this. Which is why Father captured me and started the treatments on my human form early on. The family has a small idea to what I am capable of, but they are wrong to label me what I am. You and the family see me as two separate beings. A human sister and a demon from the Banished realm when in reality, I am not. The family has forced two separate consciousnesses, when by at this stage we should be inseparable. Two forms blended into one. Instead, I am torn in two unable to be free. More so now that I am bonded to you."

It was in her last sentence I felt it through the bond.

Pain.

The feeling of being ripped in two. Tears slowly formed at the corner of my eyes, slipping down my face. The demon pushed slowly off the wall, coming in closer and lifted her hand, fingers trailing down my cheek to follow the trail my tears had taken.

"Don't cry for me, Sister."

I turned my head away in shame, only to have her grip my chin gently, forcing me to look her in the eyes. For once I did. She smiled softly, gently wiped at my tears. Shame filled my chest, as I finally understood everything.

I felt like a monster and a coward, acting how my family wanted me to— had trained me to be.

All the signs were there, they always were. This was not the first time my sister's other half tried to speak to me, and instead of allowing it, I shut down because I was a coward. What had I done all those times before?

I had run to my father, letting him know the demon was starting to take control. He would give me the look of pride I secretly coveted from him and would tell me what a good girl I was. How I made the family proud. Then he would leave to take care of my sister.

Never once did I questioned the methods being used. Never once did I think to question the family and what we did until recently, and now —now things were so much worse.

"I don't trust the families anymore." I whispered, more to myself then to the demon in front of me but it heard none the less.

The demon took a deep breath and stepped back, holding me out at an arm's length. "If this is true, then I think we can be of use to each other."

Don't miss out!

Visit the website below and you can sign up to receive emails whenever D.E. Kilgore publishes a new book. There's no charge and no obligation.

https://books2read.com/r/B-A-FXQN-UTPMB

BOOKS 2 READ

Connecting independent readers to independent writers.

About the Author

Dorothy lives in Illinois with her significant other, a boat load of turtles, and one particularly judgy lizard.

When not writing, thinking about writing, or going to reptile shows, Dorothy enjoys playing DnD and watching the scariest movies she can get her hands on.

Before launching her writing career, Dorothy received her Bachelor's degree from Northern Arizona University in Applied Anthropology with a minor in Criminal Justice.

If you would like to know more about upcoming releases, announcements, and to sign up to Dorothy's mailing list, visit her links at https://linktr.ee/authordekilgore .

Read more at https://linktr.ee/authordekilgore.

Made in the USA
Middletown, DE
03 May 2021